THE
PIRATE QUEEN

THE
PIRATE QUEEN
IN SEARCH OF THE ORBS

ILEANA DROBKIN

The Pirate Queen
In Search of the Orbs
© 2021 by Ileana Drobkin

Printed in the United States of America.
ISBN-13: 978-1-7368569-0-1
LCCN: 2021905081

Cover illustration by Jason Velasquez

CSIT Publishing
Las Vegas, Nevada

Dedication

For my Children; my inspiration,
my reason for everything!

Chapter 1

The Margola bobbed, danced and moved, as if she were a puppet on a string, serving at her master's command. Captain Sofia Bonny Rose stood in the middle of her deck, confidently calling out orders of stations to hold, while rushing to the aid of her men.

"Hold that line!" She yelled to the men, feverishly struggling to keep from losing one of the three masts.

These were the times she believed the sea was truly alive, roaring walls of water, monstrous, unforgiving and revealing its' true potential. They were in the height of the storm; the crescendo was upon *The Margola*, thrusting waves from all around in perfect harmony over her deck, forcing the ship to violently wobble one way, then back the other.

In-between the thunderous roars of the waves, a series of screams rang out as the sea reached over and snatched one of her men from the deck. Sofia leaped feet first, plunging through the volatility and into the calmer realm, where she caught site of a lifeless body. Propelling herself forward, she grabbed hold of the back of his shirt, violently kicking until they reached the surface.

"You better be alive, damn you fool!" She screamed, in-between gasps of air and working to move with the rhythm of the ocean. Just as regular breath returned, a wall of water came down over them, and she took a deep breath, dragging her man down as far below the wave as she could. When she came back to the surface, she saw a small boat belonging to *The Margola,* and it must have shaken loose from its holding during the most volatile waves. She used all she had left to reach it, kicking, knowing her life depended on it and pulling her human anchor up and down through and over the waves.

"Get in the boat! We're trying to get to you!" She instantly recognized the voice as belonging to one Louis Joseph Beaumont Mackinnon, or 'Mac' as he was known by friend and foe alike. He had a distinct accent, originally English from a noble family but growing up in-between France and Italy, he absorbed a little of both speech patterns.

"It's a good thing you aren't a big man or you'd be fish food by now." Sofia said through gritted teeth, struggling to get the small-framed body inside the little wooden boat.

She climbed in just before another wall of water poured down. She opened her eyes and by some miracle they hadn't flipped. With the wind still violently lashing the water, it had moved the little wooden boat closer to *The Margola*, and a long rope was thrown down. Rising slowly, struggling to maintain balance from the rocking, Sofia grabbed the rope, and tied it around the limp man's waist. "Pull him up!" She bellowed, cupping her hands around her mouth.

The men on board and at the other end of the rope started to chant "heave-ho" as the seemingly lifeless body rose into the dark misty air.

"What in the devil are you doing?" Shrieked Mac as he leaned over the edge, fists clenched. Several crew members grabbed the spiritless man, dragged him on board and untied him, sending the rope back overboard. The winds suddenly shifted, pushing Sofia further away from her ship, as her eyes focused on the rope and she sprang from the boat with such force it toppled over. With outstretched arms, she clutched onto the rope and held on.

"Where is she? Pull the rope! The rope! Pull it!" screamed Mac. He grabbed ahold of the rope with the men, not expecting any weight on the other end. There was weight! The men chanted "Heave-Ho, Heave-Ho…" as they pulled Sofia to them.

The men cheered, as their Captain emerged over the rail, hat in hand and grin stretching wide across her face. As quickly as the storm came upon them, it dispersed. The ship steadied, and as the waters below gently rocked back and forth in a lullaby motion, the skies transitioned from a deep grayish black to darker blue rather than speckles of bright blue.

Chapter 2

"How is he?" Sofia asked, gulping air as she made her way back on deck.

"How is he? That's the first thing you have to say!" Mac rose from kneeling beside Jessiah, second to Mac and part time healer, possessing basic skills for the wounded and sick. He was on his knees hovering over the unconscious man, checking for obvious signs of life and upon feeling the faint beating of the still unconscious man's heart, he sighed with relief. Sofia, still settling herself from her oceanic escapade, caught Mac's stern gaze and promptly turned away, shifting her attention to Jessiah.

"Jed," she knelt down next to him, "is he alive?"

Sofia was the only one on *The Margola* who referred to him as Jed.

"Aye," Jessiah set the man's hand down, "There's a pulse but he's still unconscious, Captain. Mac, will you help me move him inside." He said, glancing up to see Mac stepping towards him, giving him a slight nod in agreement.

Mac pointed at two slender but muscular men at the front of the small crowd of crew gathered around. "You two, grab the man's arms," he gathered his footing before rising and stepping aside.

"Carefully." Jessiah objected, as the men lifted his head and shoulders off the deck. "Oh, and it's nice to see ya Captain, wasn't sure we'd be seeing ya again." He smiled slightly, as he and Mac each carefully bent down and grabbed a leg. The four of them hoisted the man into the air and carefully took him inside. Some of the crew dispersed, while others loafed about, seemingly exhausted from the events of the past few hours. Sofia was leaning against the side, where she emerged, unscathed from the abyss.

As her crew scattered, she caught sight of Mac coming up from the men's quarters. His deep, hazel eyes burning, fuming as he marched up to her, "What in the bloody hell is the matter with you? You jumped overboard during a storm?" He stopped abruptly in mid thought, seeing she was smiling.

"Are you finished?" she asked, brown eyes sparkling with mischief.

"Aye, there's no point to even try, you are hell bent on getting yourself killed." He said, moving next to her, facing the ocean.

"These are my men, including you and I'm responsible, I am Captain of this ship and I don't take it lightly." She said solemnly.

"Aye..." he said, unable to counter and knowing it was futile to argue. Mac turned around, leaning his back on the rail, so he could see her face. She seemed lost within a projection of complex webs of thoughts and inner demons, as she gazed out to the sea. The awkward silence was more than he could bear. "There is something going on with you, what is it?" He asked, observing her absent-stare into the horizon.

"Sofia!" He pressed, raising his voice slightly.

"I need to tell you something. When we stopped in Barbados, I met an old woman, a fortune teller of some sort and she knew my name, she knew me. She pulled me into a back room and told me about the *Capitana Mia*."

"The Spanish royal ship, *that Capitana Mia*?" He asked, cocking his head to one side in intrigue.

"Aye, that one!"

"It's been years since it sank, what did she say about it?" He asked, hoping for information that might lead them to it and all her treasure she surely was carrying. The *Capitana Mia* was a royal Spanish vessel, rumored to have been transporting chests of jewels and gold.

"She said the ship held answers of who my parents were and there's some type of magical orb that was my destiny."

Mac looked over at her and she caught his gaze, smiling slightly, knowing he was with her on this newest adventure to find the orb on the *Capitana Mia*. For a moment, they stood watching the horizon, not a word spoken between them.

Sophia bit the bottom of her lip in reflective thought before clearing her throat,

"She mentioned there's another amongst us who knows of the orb's existence and it's power. An evil man, one with a black heart." She said slowly and barely audible.

"Captain Tyberias "Black Heart" Keen!" Mac slowly annunciated each part of his name with disgust. "Across the vastness of the oceans and in all the lands, we keep running into Black Heart! I don't think it's much of a coincidence! We obviously have a destiny to meet!"

His words foreboding, yet overtones of optimism in his voice gave her hope of putting some finality on old Captain Black Heart. Maybe she would finally discover who her parents were and why they were aboard the doomed ship without her.

Black Heart was obsessed with Sofia, ever since their very first encounter, when he thought she was a man. She stood almost six feet tall, muscularly feminine build with a mental presence harmonious with her appearance. She was intimidating, an unexpected force of nature, generally rendering her foes speechless and awestricken long enough for her to seize the tactical advantage. She was one of only a handful of pirate women who was as fierce and formidable as any man.

"Aye, I think he's afraid of you most!" He said turning to Sofia.

She made a funny noise, sounding somewhere in-between a giggle and a grunt, "I think he's afraid the afterlife won't be kind to him if he were killed by a woman!"

Keen once murdered several of her crew, while in port in Nassau, leaving taunting messages on the bodies. Not long after, he sent two of his men to stalk her on Port Royal, Jamaica, attempting to grab her outside of one of her haunts but she overpowered both of them, sending them back with broken bones and a story to tell. He was ruthless and feared by pirates and everyday citizens alike, but not Sofia, she didn't fear him at all and that drove him mad! She consumed his every waking thought and became the motivation for every move he made. She was confident she could kill him if the opportunity arose, but she knew if she were a man, their game of cat and mouse would have ended long ago. They stood in silence, each digesting the information, watching the sea completely transition to tranquility.

Chapter 3

Sofia entered the sick area of the ship to check on her rescue.

"Captain, you've come at a good time, he's conscious and talking." smiled Jessiah, delighted with his healing skills. She nodded, timidly stepping up to the man's bedside.

"Captain Rose, I thank you for saving my life." The man uttered hoarsely.

She smiled, slightly embarrassed not knowing the man's name. "Your name sailor?" She asked abruptly.

"Henry William Longfellow, Captain," the man struggling to rise, resting on his elbows.

"You speak rather perfect English, if you don't mind me saying, you don't seem the usual pirate." She took a couple of steps back, folding her arms.

"My family are educators; I am an educated man and a writer. Mostly poetry at the moment. I joined your crew months ago in hopes of gaining experiences to write about." He said, laying back down, exhausted.

"I've had a lot of crew but never a writer!" She said, creases of her mouth inching upwards. "Henry William Longfellow, that's a regal name if I ever heard one. Do you want to go back home, Henry?" She asked, secretly hoping he would realize he wasn't up to the natural pirate ventures.

"If it's all the same to you Captain Rose, I'd like to stay onboard."

She nodded slowly, smiling, "Jed, you are in charge of Mr. Longfellow's safety, as long as he so chooses to grace us with his presence." She sprouted a wide Cheshire grin, "Poet turned pirate, aye, well that may not be so bad. The possibilities, the history—" She trailed off, eyes sparkling, lost to thought.

Her words were laced with such joy, Jessiah suppressed the urge to laugh. "Aye, Captain, I shall make sure Mr. Longfellow is out of harm's way but experiences enough of a pirate life to write about us."

"I thank you, Captain Rose." Mr. Longfellow uttered, closing his eyes, creases of his mouth slightly turned upwards.

She gave Jessiah a slight nod, long damp tangled strands of hair covering part of her grin. She glanced back over at Mr. Longfellow as she turned to leave; his eyes closed, chest rising and falling in peaceful, rhythmic movements. Her smile faded, as she climbed the stairs back to the deck, consumed by the fortuneteller's words, generating questions, though she had no answers; how her destiny involved a magical orb of some sort and how did Tyberias "Black Heart" Keen come upon the knowledge of the existence of this orb.

❈ ❈ ❈

Sofia was barely 16 when she found her way to Portsmouth. Dawning men's pants, hair tucked into the back of a large painter's shirt and a man's three-point hat, she did her best to blend into the drinking establishment. Taking a seat at a small table in the very back corner of the room, looking up in brief intervals as to not catch any gaze of the less than desirable characters. As she looked up, she caught the gaze of a large, bedraggled, portly man. His black hair and black beard had strands of silver woven throughout.

She readied herself for whatever this encounter

would present, and felt a rumbling of excitement within her stomach at the possibility. This was the beginning of a whole new world for her.

She looked down at her glass as he started moving towards her. This was the first time she'd been away from home. While she'd experienced a typical girl's upbringing; she was born different. There was more than a touch of saltwater coursing through her veins. The love and ease she experienced with a sword made her born for a pirates' life.

"Are ya looking for a ship to sail lad?"

Sofia tilted her head slightly, sizing up the black-haired pirate. He stood around her height, overweight but muscular and an air of smugness and moral turpitude wafted around him.

Before Sofia was able to formulate an answer, the man grabbed the seat across from her and sat himself down. "Well, are ya?" He pushed gruffly. He glared across the table, sizing her up.

Attempting her most manly voice, "That depends, what are you offering?"

"Room and board and a percentage of the loot."

"What's the percentage?" Sofia could feel the

man's gaze becoming more intense, compelling her to look up.

"My crew doesn't complain about what they get." He answered tersely.

"I bet they don't." she quipped.

Angry and agitated, the black-bearded man stood and drew his sword, drawing the attention of the establishment's patrons.

She rose slowly, unveiling her true size, dawning a menacing gaze. "My answer is no and you'd be best served to leave my presence!" Sofia kept a close eye on the man's sword, not showing any signs in the least of yielding. During the short encounter with the man, she had moved her dirk from her waist into the sleeve of her right hand. Her sword in its' sheath, dangling from her hip, as she contemplated her next moves, as a first-time, self-proclaimed pirate engaged in battle with what she surmised was a genuine pirate.

There was now a small crowd gathered around them as though the final round of a chess game was in play. "No person living challenges Captain Tyberias Keen!" he shouted in a crazed episode.

"Challenged?" Sofia laughed, "This deranged outburst is because I wanted to know the terms, should I come to work on your ship!" She laughed again, although with some restraint, as she appreciated her surroundings and this pirate's unstable nature. She saw the motion of the dagger but couldn't react in time. A burning sensation ignited below her right shoulder, as blood ran down her arm, seeping through and staining her shirt. Showing no emotion, she swiftly transferred her dirk into her right hand and used her left hand to pull his dagger from her bloody right sleeve, then threw it onto the floor behind her.

"Leave!" She ordered, voice calm and controlled, as she transferred her dagger back into her left hand.

"Ha, ha!" the black-bearded pirate laughed maniacally. "I shall see you dead first!" He barked back, sword in hand. Without warning, he lunged at Sofia, his sword scraping against the dagger in her left hand. She held back his attack with just the dagger, having no warning nor the knowledge to pull her sword.

"That's quite enough!" Said a young man. As Keen swung back his sword to strike Sofia once more, the young man snuck his sword to the back of Captain Keen. "Leave him be Captain!" he said, eyeing Sofia, having no reason not to believe between her size, sheer strength and brashness that she was not a he.

Sofia's sudden movements in the struggle loosened her hat from her head. As she shifted her weight, her hat fell to the ground and her hair came loose, wavy strands of luscious brown hair flowing off her shoulders.

"You're a bloody woman!" Exclaimed Captain Keen. Clearly more agitated, he lunged at her again, but this time Sofia moved back and to the left. The young man reflexively caught Keen by his sword belt, giving Sofia enough time to pull her sword from its' sheath hanging on her hip. There was an audible gasp from onlookers, as there were the occasional women who dressed as men to drink without question or bother. But, never had anyone seen a woman speak with such command.

"Aye, I'm a woman!" Sofia laughed, steadying the sword in her left hand, as blood continued trickling down her dominant right hand. She had spent a great deal of time learning to fight with both hands, if the need should ever arise, and was quite capable and comfortable left-handed. The black-bearded captain was craftier with a sword than his looks conveyed. He swung around in one giant motion, forcing the young man to lose his grip on the sword belt. But the young man proved a master of agility, leaping backwards; giving him enough time to ready himself. The captain advanced towards him, as the young man's sword swung wildly, blocking the onslaught.

After several minutes of fierce swordplay, Keen stopped as abruptly as he began, "I have no time for you, Mac!" He shouted angrily, so confident in his knowledge of the young man that he spun around with no fear of a dagger or sword to his back and refocused his wrath.

Keen fixed his murderous gaze on Sofia; advanced age and a rotund body starved solely of exercise forced him to physically halt his pursuit and grab the back of a wooden chair. His large body resting at a tilt on his long muscularly, flabby arm, as he slowed his mouth breathing; waiting for the opportune moment to strike.

"Can you fight?" the young man asked, moving around Keen, close enough for Sofia to decipher but outside Keen's peripheral scope.

Sofia nodded slightly, keeping Keen's gaze. Not knowing who this young man was and why he was risking himself for her sake, was a mystery to her. Added to the mystery was why she was instantly taken with him, trusted him without knowing so much as his name. He's nice looking and fair with a sword she thought to herself, as she waited for her moment to strike.

There was a glimmer in Keen's eyes, a spark of the devil, his mouth turned upwards, bursting open with glee, revealing gray and rotting teeth, as he lifted his plump pointer finger in the air. "Kill her!"

Keen's men moved forward towards Sofia, some with swords at the ready, others baulking at the idea of fighting a woman, a young one at that. Neither the crew nor Keen paid any mind to the young man, who tactfully stayed out of Keen's line of sight, so it took the black-hearted captain by surprise when the young man who served under him for a short time, again stepped in to challenge him.

"Keen, you better tell your crew to back up." He said, while driving the sword's point into the pirate's back. Sofia held her position, sword at the ready in her left hand and her dagger in her right, as blood continued to streak down her arm and hand. Her eyes shifted from Keen to the rough-looking characters just feet from her. The young man whipped around with his flailing captive and backed up slowly, so he was just in front of Sofia.

"Ya know me well enough my boy, I won't give ya satisfaction," Captain Black Heart said; turning his head slightly to one side.

"Get back!" He ordered, "Get back and no harm will come to your captain." He jabbed the dagger deeper into the elder pirate's coat.

The men looked to their captain for guidance but received nothing. Keen, thinking he had the upper hand, was suddenly too stunned for anything but playing the part of the captive. With that, the young man hastily gave Keen a hardy shove, drew back his long leg and kicked the stout pirate, sending him flying towards his motley crew of thugs. With sword in hand, Sofia sprang from the corner like a wound-up Jack in the Box, lunging and extending her left arm, just able to make a nice slice in the side of his blubbering belly.

"Damn ya woman!" He hollered, followed by a series of expletives foreign to Sofia's young ears. Sofia sprung back, putting distance between her and the wounded captain, as she caught a glimpse of the young man locking swords and outnumbered by Keen's men. Sofia joined in the fight, working to control the rhythm and pace leading her foes, two and three at a time, into a hypnotic death dance.

"She's just a bloody woman!" Keen screamed indignantly, as he held his bleeding belly; lifted himself upright and leaned against a wall.

"Aye! One they've never seen the likes of." She shouted back, as a mischievous grin spread wide across her face. Injured himself, with only two men left on their feet, the captain ordered the men to help him to his ship; refusing to use the word retreat. He caught Sofia's gaze, forbidding and so intense it sent a small shiver up his black-hearted spine. Sofia held his gaze until he pulled his eyes, leaving wounded in body and spirit. She scanned the room through blurred vision, her painter's shirt soaked with blood from her wounded shoulder. With the room absent of threats, her adrenaline soon faded and she fell where she stood.

Chapter 4

"Where the devil am I?" Sofia sat up wincing in pain, as she grabbed her wounded arm, now wrapped in strips of cloth.

"Don't move, you're safe," said the young man from the pub.

"Where am I?"

"My room," he smiled timidly.

"We were never formally introduced," she said, easing back down on the bed.

"Ah, yes, Louis Joseph Beaumont Mackinnon, but I go by Mac."

"Well, thank you, Mac," she smiled, momentarily forgetting the throbbing pain rushing through her arm.

"And what do they call you? You're obviously not a man and I've not seen anyone fight quite like you!"

She slowly pulled herself up to a sitting position, "I'm Sofia Bonny Rose and no I'm certainly not a man!"

Mac stood at a distance so not to startle her, although after seeing her fight, he was more afraid of what she could do to him if she felt he was a threat. "What in all that is holy were you doing at that pub and alone?" He crossed his arms, anticipating some half-baked concoction of a story, seeing as she was very young and clearly wanting to disguise her sexual identity.

"I'm actually not sure, to tell you the truth. I've run away from home to sail on the seas and thought I could—"

"Find someone willing to take you on at the pub?" He interrupted before she could finish the sentence, laughing at the absurdity of it all but stopping in mid chuckle. "Do you know who that pirate is?"

"Well, I didn't stop to ask him his name, while he was on his way out." she replied sarcastically.

"Captain Tyberias "Black Heart" Keen!" He unfolded his arms and began pacing.

"Black Heart?" Everyone had heard of Black Heart. He was one of the most notoriously ruthless pirates around. The stories of his infamous murderous rages spread through her town, as it had through all of England and its' colonies. "Hmm," she thought, pursing her lips together, "I rather thought he would have been much more terrifying and a far better fighter. I found him a bit pathetic, actually."

Mac stopped pacing, turned facing Sofia dawning a look of both shock and amazement at the words coming out of this young woman's mouth. He left her comments unanswered, sensing there was nothing he could say for her to think otherwise.

"You had run-ins with him before? You knew his name and it seemed he knew you." She was trying to make sense of the previous chaotic hours.

"I was one of his crew for a short time, a *very short* time." He put great emphasis on "very short". "I didn't like the way he operated, and I do not like to harm people, if it's not necessary."

"And Black Heart does." She added, dispassionately.

"That he does, so I left and came back home."

She sighed and felt around the wrapping of her wound, "Did someone sew me up?"

"I did." He said, pleased with his abilities for stitching wounds. "Where did you learn to fight like that?" He crossed his arms again, this time anticipating a much fuller answer than the previous.

"Family friend, a Scot, he was a master swordsman and I went to stay with him and his family for a year."

"He taught you to fight with both hands?"

She laughed until she felt a series of pains running down her arm. "I took to the sword rather quickly, so he thought it prudent I should become just as comfortable with my left hand."

He stepped closer to her and knelt down beside the bed. "How are you feeling?"

The creases on both sides of her full, red lips turned upwards, stretching into a smile. "You'd make a fine tailor!"

She settled herself back down on the pillow and promptly fell to sleep. She stayed a few days before parting ways with him, taking leave in the dark of night. She left a note assuring him they were destined to meet again, serendipitously, two years later they did on *The Margola*.

※ ※ ※

Chapter 5

"Ship…Ship…Ship!" Jessiah yelled from the crow's nest.

Weeks of daily duties to maintain the ship amongst blue sky and sea in every direction had no doubt worn on every last crew member. As the words fell down upon the deck, every man on board rushed about to see where the ship had been spotted.

Sofia and Mac ran on deck. They had spent day after day combing over possible routes the *Capitana Mia* could have taken. "To your stations!" She shouted, as she ran towards the crow's nest. "Can you see the type of flag?"

"Not yet Captain." The deck became eerily silent, not one sound made by a single sailor, all eyes and ears waiting for direction, the smell of adrenaline permeating the warm air.

"British flag, Captain, it's a British flag!" Yelled Jessiah, eyes intently focused on the detailed prying of a spyglass.

She grabbed one of the men closest to her "Get the British flag up now!" They sailed with a healthy variety of flags representing differing nations, diverse messages including a pirate flag and white flag of truce.

"Clever!" Yelled Mac, handing out weapons to the crew. This was not their first battle and most of this crew had been with them for long enough to know their positions and roles. Their movements readying for battle were seamlessly choreographed with sailors falling in lockstep with one another, harmonizing in clanks and bangs of weapons. The ship was now closing in and just as Sofia looked up to yell for Jed to get down, his body swung through the air with the greatest ease and landed with a simple audible thud next to her.

"Show Off!" She smiled, as he tipped his hat and ran to his station. The invading ship seemed to slow some with the presence of the British flag now flying from *The Margola*'s mast. Sofia stood just out of sight but if they were boarded, she made sure she was the first thing the intruders would come to. She lived for these moments and showed little nerves and little fear.

A thunderous bang echoed, as the boarding plank hit their deck and moments later a stout, black-bearded beast of a man came across, staring straight at Sofia. "Bloody woman!" He spit with indignation on the deck.

There was little shock from Sofia or her crew on the presence of Captain "Black Heart" Keen and his pirates, as they had hunted Sofia and her crew on land and boarded *The Margola* several times; flying differing flags as a disguise. Each encounter costing *The Margola* men and lost time in trade and plundering but always proving Sofia a formidable opponent and giving the black-hearted captain perverse joy in his entanglement with the only female pirate captain.

Sofia didn't blink, just held her gun in ready position, eyeing the middle of the grotesque human squawking before her. "Get off my ship Keen or I will blow a hole the size of Nassau in you!" She didn't know why she didn't outright end him right there. Her tone of voice and unwavering stance forced Captain Keen backwards by a few steps, as he suddenly motioned his hand, and a wave of men came rushing over the gangplank. Sofia shot the first sailor wielding a sword aiming to strike her down, then quickly put the gun back in her waist and drew her sword. Most were no match for her expert skills with a sword, as she fell back further onto the ship, stabbing and jousting one after another. Under orders from their Captain, three of Keen's men quickly advanced on their target, Sofia had her back towards them as she fended off another two.

"Sofia, behind you!" Jessiah and Mac yelled in unison, catching her attention just in time for Sofia to stop playing around, slash the two men and turn her attention to the advancing three foes.

A blast of gunfire erupted from one side of the ship to the other, but *The Margola*'s crew always maintained the upper hand when attacked on their ship. They had a reputation for setting traps and were very successful at defending their ship! Those belonging to Captain Keen, who were alive and able-bodied, threw themselves overboard or made a calculated attempt to return back to their ship. Mac and Jessiah rushed over to help their Captain, "Can one of you at least take one of these sorry excuses for men?"

Jessiah tapped the shorter and thinner one on the shoulder, drawing his immediate attention. "Now kid, back to your ship with you and I won't harm you." Jessiah figured he was not much younger than himself and really didn't want to kill the poor bastard.

"No, sir I will not!" said the kid in a British accent.

Moments later, Jessiah was standing over the young Brit, supporting a sword to his neck. Leaning into him further, forcing the blade to now touch his neck, "This is your last chance, return to your ship and go back to your family!"

The sailor nodded, Jessiah gripped the boy's sword in one hand and his in the other. Slowly, he let the sailor up and escorted him off *The Margola*. Meanwhile, Mac was proudly leaning on the railing, relaxed as if he were watching some sporting event, cheering Sofia on. "Oh, just get rid of them already, it's been a long day."

Finally, having enough, her eyes narrowed, she affirmed her grip on her blade and finished one off and turned slightly to face the last of the standing enemy crew. He backed up, dropping the sword and begged for his life.

"Go!" Sofia kept an eye on the man, while she slowly bent down to pick up his sword, "Go!" She yelled again. The man took a couple more steps backwards, then turned on his heels and ran like the wind over the gangplank. She stepped back, veins throbbing with sharp electrical waves running throughout her body, as she tightened her grip on the blood-covered sword. She gasped for air, in deep but shallow breaths, feeling as though she was drowning in the watery depths below. The enemy ship, along with Captain Keen, had pulled away, just as the pirate she allowed to escape ran across the gangplank. She dropped her sword and pulled her long hair out from the back of her shirt, soaked from hours of continued rapid movements. She fell back onto the deck, resting her weary extremities. Sofia slowly rose, taking stock of herself, then shifting attention to her crew and ship. "Thanks for your help."

Mac turned, revealing a smile. "They were no match for you, you didn't need me."

"Would you have just let them get the best of me then, three to one?" Her tone harboring only a hint of annoyance but a fair amount of sarcasm.

"I was there in case you needed me, none of those jokers had much training with a blade."

Tired of the conversation, she changed course "Did we lose anyone, anyone hurt?"

"A couple with some flesh wounds, some bruises but looks like everyone made it through."

Relieved at the news, Sofia was looking around the ship, although too mentally and physically drained to take proper stock herself, she relied on Mac and Jessiah to conduct the post-battle inventory. There was some damage but mostly cosmetic or temporarily repairable with what they had on board.

Chapter 6

Sofia started to pace around the desk, set in the middle of her quarters, tapping her fingers as she moved in hypnotic circles. "Why would Keen attack and not make bloody sure we were swallowed up by the sea or, at the very least, make sure I was removed from this world?"

She asked the question out loud again and again, expecting the answer to appear. They had gone up against Keen several times before and it was never easy or pleasant. Keen's men were bloodthirsty and trained, not anything like the crew who just attacked. She abruptly halted the hypnotic pacing and stood over the table, head slumped down, her long, luxuriant, wavy, brown hair falling onto the table. "Oh god!" she exclaimed softly, instantly realizing a game of cat and mouse was in play and she was the cat, playing in the hands of the orchestrator. "It was all a set-up!" She whispered, exhaling simultaneously. She felt the blood drain from her head, her heart pounded harder and faster, and as she tried to stand up, her legs gave way under duress.

❈ ❈ ❈

"Sofia! Sofia! Can you hear me?"

She opened one amber, lash-studded eye, then the other, completely aware, utterly embarrassed and thoroughly infuriated she was found in this state. She felt to the sides of her, feeling the wooden floorboards beneath her and gingerly sat up, using her hands to steady herself.

"You ok, Captain?" Jessiah, was bending over staring at her, unsure what to make of it. He and the rest of the crew seldom saw her in a vulnerable position.

"I'm fine, Jed." she stammered, as she labored, getting her legs beneath her. As she stood, steadying herself, a large hand grabbed onto her and pulled her up the rest of the way. Even when she stood erect and seemed stable, Mac held onto her, both holding each other's gaze. There were very few times Mac asserted real control, especially over Sofia, but upon the rare occasion she didn't fight it, she even seemed to enjoy the change and challenge it presented.

"You can let me go now!" Her voice barely audible to the small crowd gathered in her quarters.

"Get back to work everyone! The Captain is fine," he ordered, without breaking his gaze or moving a muscle. Once the door shut behind the last of the crew Mac let go, "What happened? You all right?"

She nodded, massaging her temples with her long fingers.

"It was a set-up..." she sighed quietly and quickly looked down. "I was thinking that too. That wasn't his usual crew."

She looked up with a slight upward turn of her full, red lips pressing into a smile, relieved they were on the same wave-length. "It was a set up but for what and how?" Sofia sat down, while Mac leaned against the wall across from her. "What if the attack was meant for a distraction?"

Mac quickly stood up, "The cargo hold!"

They both bolted for the door, moving so quickly the wooden door shed small pieces of its' wood as it slammed on the wall in the corridor. Sofia and Mac dashed down to the cargo hold, swords out. Once they reached the stairs, leading down to the vast cargo hold, they slowed their pace and lightened their footing. Slits of light peered into the hold through the cracks in the wooden planks above, as the sun was beginning its decent, ending what had been a very long day. There was just enough light coming in for them to see inches in front of them. Mac stopped suddenly, holding up his hand for Sofia to see and stop behind him.

There was a rhythmic humming from beneath them, as the waves gently moved the ship up and down and lapping the wooden planks from one side to the other. They stood in silence, barely breathing, listening, stalking, hunting and there it was, a slight rustling noise.

"Show yourself!" Mac extended his sword, as an extension of his body.

A short shadow slowly moved from behind a large crate, "Please don't kill me," said the shadow. The voice was young, obviously scared and by itself. Mac grabbed the shadow, as Sofia turned back through the narrow path, now leading the three of them to the stairs and into the light of the deck.

Chapter 7

Back on the twilight-lit deck, a crowd of crew members now circled the would-be spy, while Sofia took center stage in the questioning with Mac beside her. "I am Sofia Bonny Rose, Captain of *The Margola*, the ship where you now stand. Who are you? Why are you here?"

The short, gangly figure couldn't be more than 14 years old, with red, wavy hair and sparkling, blue eyes and he shook uncontrollably, as he opened his small, thin-lipped mouth to speak but not a single syllable rolled off his tongue.

Sofia signed and lowered her sword, "No harm is going to come to you, boy. Answer my questions!"

After a minute or so of what can only be described as a gathering of courage, the boy opened his mouth, "I'm called Red, my given name is Alexander Angus Ridell Stewart. I was taken by Captain Keen from my home in Scotland and told to hide below, until ye found the orb, then I was supposed to steal it from ye and meet back on Nassau!" There was no hiding that Scottish brogue or that ginger topping.

"You just obeyed, then followed orders of a man who kidnapped you?" Sofia asked, softening her tone.

"No madam!"

"Captain!" Mac snapped sharply at the boy.

"Beg your pardon, Captain. He told me he would go and find my family and kill them all, while making me watch. Then he would kill me, if I didn't do as I was told."

"That sounds like the Keen we know and distain." Mac said, without a hint of surprise.

"Why would Keen send a child to steal something so rare…" she thought for a moment, thinking out loud, "Why would he think a child could pull something like that in front of me, in front of my crew?" She paced up and down in front of the would-be spy, like a pendulum, up one way and right back the other.

"Captain Keen said he will'na mess with ye until he has the orb." the would-be spy added.

Sofia stopped at that added piece of knowledge,

"What does he know about the orb?" Sofia asked, stopping directly in front of the young Scot.

"Only that you want it…" he was forming the word to say Miss, when he caught Mac's gaze and promptly added, with a slight delay, "Captain!"

Something still bothered Sofia, she couldn't figure out his crew. That wasn't his usual crew, they were fierce fighters, they were ruthless, and cutthroat but those on display earlier were none of that. She put those thoughts aside, dealing with the more immediate issues.

"I'm done with the questions and answers, tell us the entire plan or so help me you won't see a tomorrow!" Sofia pulled her dirk out of her waist and held it to the boy's pale, thin neck. Red drew in a breath, trying to control his shaking, and the light reddish hairs on his arms stood at attention, while his knees showed signs of buckling.

"Tell us everything and no harm will come to you," Mac moved close to the boy, gently touching his shoulder.

Red slowly exhaled and nervously looked down at the deck, "Keen knows about the black pirate,

Apollo and ye, I overheard him saying he wants the power of ye both and the orb!" The ginger-haired boy exhaled slowly, relieved of the burden as life of a spy. Sofia pulled back the dirk and placed it back into her waistband, not fully secure in understanding what her connection to Apollo meant and what power Keen was referring to.

"Jed, take him and get him something to eat but watch him," Sofia ordered. Jessiah nodded, grabbed the boy by his tattered, collared shirt and led him down to the kitchen. The crowd dispersed with Jessiah and the would-be spy, leaving Sofia and Mac alone on the dimly lit deck.

Chapter 8

Sofia walked over to the side of the ship, hung her head down into her sizable hands, feeling not only the ample weight of command but the overwhelming burden of an arch nemesis. Mac walked over and leaned with his back against the side, "What do ya think Keen is up to?"

"Keen knows about the orb and knows about Apollo but I don't have the foggiest how I'm connected to the black ghost." She sighed, still not looking up. Apollo had become an enigma; his fighting prowess was legendary, both on sea and land. He, a known and feared pirate for 30 years and she a young captain, of only a few.

Mac nodded, even though Sofia's face remained buried. "Thank all that is holy, he sent a boy to do a man's job!" He said knowing that would get a rise out of Sofia and trying to lighten the mood.

"Oh, a man's job," Sofia lifted her head, turning to Mac, with a fiery gaze. Mac reflexively opened his mouth in retort but quickly closed it, pressing his top teeth into his bottom lip. He meant it to lighten the situation but, clearly, she took it to heart. His eyes narrowed at the provocateur next to him, as he took the moment to gather his thoughts to avoid venturing down the proverbial rabbit's hole, she was so good at luring him into. He took a deep breath and, not as calm as he was hoping, expressed "Yes, a man's job and you know very well when I refer to a man's job and a woman's, it doesn't pertain to you. I don't know why you always have to bring yourself into it and you know exactly what I mean!"

She suppressed the urge to laugh, hiding her smile within the cup of her hands. Being a woman who had a remarkable amount of commonly noted masculine attributes, and who performed many of the most noted manly duties just as well and, in some cases, far superior to most men, she took great pleasure in ribbing him on what constituted the make-up of a man and the duties associated. Mac was all too well aware and she knew that.

Where most men objected to her crossing the traditional lines of feminine rolls, Mac liked and loved her for it. However, much as Sofia wasn't like most women of her time, Mac certainly wasn't like most men. They were a pair made for one another, transcending stereotypical gender roles, enlightened, educated and woke! Choosing a life of piracy was not for the faint of heart but choosing it as a woman and one who refused to hide her femininity was topsy turvy. The challenge of her, for him, was of a moth to a flame, completely irresistible ending with a high likelihood of injury or death.

They stood in awkward silence for a time, thoughts returning to the dire issue at hand and to find The *Capitana Mia* and the orb, all while evading Black Heart.

"We don't have much of a choice..." Sofia started, mind racing with unanswered questions, "All roads lead back to The *Capitana Mia* and the orb."

Mac nodded slowly. "Keen has a network of ruthless pirates, both friends and enemies, all willing to sell their own mothers for a bit of gold." Mac was quick to point that out, having his own not-to-pleasant encounters with Black Heart and his crew.

"True." She uttered, with a slight nod of her head.

❆ ❆ ❆

Maps of port cities and ocean charts adorned a long table in Sofia's quarters, as she studiously went from one to the other, weighing their options and playing out scenarios in her head. Keen's obsession and pursuit was bound to come to a head and with the information from the would-be spy, they found themselves in position to turn the tables on the black-hearted pirate. Immersed in the train of maps, Sofia never heard Mac come into the room and stand beside her. "We could stop in Barbados; we shouldn't be very far."

Sofia's right hand was busy rummaging through her long, auburn hair, something she did when she had nervous energy flowing through her. "I was thinking the same, in fact there are a couple of, um, pirates we can pick up." she had a mischievous look in her eyes and muffled a series of giggles.

Mac sighed, instantly realizing who the 'um, pirates' she was referring to were. Benny and Hugh, as cunning and clever as they were mischievous, working in concert to drive even the most hardened human up the crow's nest.

"Why?" Head cocked; Mac shot Sofia a piercing glance. She caught a glimpse of his glance and turned her head sharply away.

Matching his weighty tone, "They are expert swordsmen and superb fighters. You know very well we can use the help and unlike most ships, we run a very slim crew. Keen's crew is nearly double what we have, and I would not put it past him to recruit mercenaries to ensure our demise."

Mac grumbled and said something in Latin, his preferred language when irritated or mad, "*nos autem non in deo cara est!*"

"Dear God we are in for it now." Sofia interpreted and shot him a look rivaling his.

Mac shook his head. "Those two are insufferable! Each and every time those two are on this ship, they wreak havoc! They drink the wine and whiskey meant for sale and make general nuisances out of themselves." Sofia watched in amusement as Mac spent the next several minutes pacing and mumbling things to himself. Benny and Hugh certainly made things livelier on a ship. Their skill with blades and hand-to-hand combat far outweighed their antics.

Chapter 9

They sailed into the port of Bridgetown, Barbados, as an emulsion of scintillating colors stained the sky over the small triangular-shaped island. Wanting to avoid any and all distractions, Sofia slipped off the ship, without detection, and headed to the tavern most known for the "unsavory" type.

Inside the tavern, she walked slowly, searching for the Scotsman and Irishman duo; a hand reached out and pulled her into a dimly-lit room. Before Sofia could respond in any kind of way, the hand let go. Her eyes fixed on the large figure sitting at a table near the end of the small room, enveloped by particles of dust and light making their way through the crevices.

"Sofia, I am Apollo!" The figure said in a deep and smooth baritone voice.

"How do you know my name?"

Apollo leaned forward into the light, allowing Sofia to see more of his features. Even seated, she could tell he was a tall, strapping black man with deep set, dark eyes and a long-jagged scar, resembling a lightning bolt, running from his right eyebrow to his cheek. She maintained a steely gaze, frozen in time like a statue.

"How do you know my name?" She demanded once more.

Apollo's eyes sparkled; the corners of his mouth drew into a smile, as he sat back into the shadows. "I've known you since you sailed for your very first time." he said, with a hint of mystery in his velvet, melodious voice.

"That's not—" she stopped, as he put his right hand in the air, apparently a signal for her to cease.

"I understand you are looking for pirates named Benny and Hugh." Just as he finished saying their names, the men appeared through the door Sofia was pushed through. "There is much you don't know but all will be revealed in time. Go now!"

Sofia looked over at the two men standing by the door and turned back in Apollo's direction but the black pirate had slipped out of a passageway behind his chair. Both male figures stepped in unison into the beams of light, showing themselves to Sofia.

Benny dwarfed Hugh by several inches and was proportionally thin, while Hugh was an inch or so smaller than Sofia but brawny in mass.

"Lass!" Both dark-haired, brown-eyed men declared excitedly in unison. Sofia barely had time for a quick smile before the two men descended upon her in a lengthy embrace.

"You're with Apollo?" She asked, not directing the question to either of them in particular.

"Aye, we are that lass and have been since the last time we parted." Hugh replied in his most eloquent Scottish brogue.

Despite their different heritage, Hugh from Scotland and Benny from Ireland, the two had been inseparable since they were in their early teenaged years, when they both had run away from home to answer the call of romance and adventure, paired with sea life.

"Who is Apollo and how does he know me?" Sofia shook her head, "I don't understand any of this!"

Hugh and Benny looked at one another, Hugh nodded, "He's a good one, Apollo, I mean. He's fair-minded and a good Captain."

Sofia gave a half smile and nodded, genuinely happy the boys found a home, although she'd never known them to stay with a ship for a lengthy time. "If you're with Apollo, why are you here with me?"

The men looked at one another again. "Apollo heard you were looking for Benny and me and he knows you can use the help." said Hugh.

"We are at your service." Benny added.

She looked at the two men, slowly shaking her head back and forth drowning to the mounting waves of frustration flowing inside her. Reflexively, she balled both her fists and the slight smile she dawned moments earlier flatlined, as she took a healthy amount of air through her nose and let out a slow and steady breath.

"Ok, I'm going to try and ask you two again, who is Apollo and how does he know me?" She was out of breath by the end of the question.

Hugh and Benny looked at one another again, they seemed to have an unspoken language all their own. Hugh sighed and took a couple of steps back, unsure how she was going to receive what he was about to convey. "Apollo snuck on a ship when he was a young man and rose through the ranks to Captain of The *Reckoning*. In between serving you on *The Margola*, Benny and I serve aboard The *Reckoning* and have for years."

Sofia's eyes narrowed, as she steadied herself against the back wall of the room but motioned for Hugh to continue. He cleared his throat, "You see, lass, Apollo has been keeping tabs on ya since the day ya found home on the sea. He gave his word to your parents to see ya safe."

At the mention of her parents, Sofia looked up, eyes wide with emotion. "My parents? They drowned on a vessel heading to the colonies when I was too young to remember them. Did Apollo know my parents?" The question was more for the universe to answer as the two men stood there in awkward silence.

Chapter 10

Back aboard *The Margola*, Sofia's mind wandered to the first time she met Hugh and Benny…

The Margola was in port at Bridgetown. Its' captain making trades and deals for the transporting of rum to Nassau. She preferred venturing into town alone and often slipped away from the "guards" Mac ordered to escort her. They generally spent much of their time on land searching for her, generally tracing her whereabouts several hours behind. Sofia attracted trouble, she sought it out, she welcomed it and she relished it when it came. As if her height alone wasn't enough to cause heads to turn, she adorned a sword on one side of her hip and a dirk on the other over pants and knee-high boots with her long hair flowing in the open. She strutted down the street with the confidence of 10 men and held a smirk on her face as men, women and children ogled her. She was a force of great admiration but also of great persecution for, after all, women of the time didn't look or act as she.

Sofia sat at a table in the back of a pub across from Tobias Jansen, a Jewish/Dutch man whom acted as an intermediary for producers of rum and the paying customer.

Tobias, a small, thin man with light features was a very serious man. He was neither loyal nor opportunistic, rather any agreement made was an agreement honored. He took no issues with Captain Sofia Bonny Rose, all he cared was that she had kept her end of the agreement before and he believed she would do so again. Upon a handshake agreement, Tobias rose, bidding Sofia goodbye with a tip of his hat. As he turned on heels to leave, a large plump finger stuck in the small man's chest.

"Where do ye think ye be going?" Said a towering figure, as tall as he was round. The man had several teeth missing and a black patch covered his right eye, forcing him to cock his head slightly to the right. "I want the rum ye speak of. All of it!" He barked, spewing spit from his foaming mouth.

Tobias, dwarfed almost a foot by the fowl-smelling man, was braver than his looks revealed, as he stood, eyes following the plump, dirt-ridden finger up to the dirt-ridden face of its' owner. "I have things to do sir and we do not have an agreement. My agreement is with the Captain." said Tobias, pointing over to Sofia without taking his eyes off of the towering, portly man.

The man grunted and plunged his finger into Tobias' chest, "I don't think ye be understanding, I'm going to have your rum, whether ye be dead or not!"

Sofia sat watching Tobias' every move, waiting for a sign to step in, as it was not considered good manners to do so on another man's battle and embarrass them. Tobias, always with the same expressionless face, and never showing signs of joy, fear, or anger, stared straight into the grotesque man's face. "Sir, I have no intention of giving you even one drop of the rum."

The man turned shades of red with anger, but Tobias didn't move an inch, rather held up his left hand as some kind of signal. Sofia quickly got to her feet, sword out and ready, but the signal was not meant for her intervention. Before anyone could make a move, two pirates flanked the large man with the tips of their dirks touching, but not piercing the shirt covering the flabby flesh of his middle.

"Aye, I don't think that's a good idea, Jack." Said the taller man with the corn-silk, blond hair and discernible Scottish brogue.

Jack, although not the brightest of pirates, apparently knew it was best to never travel alone. He gave a rather booming grunt and with that came several armed, fowl-smelling pirates forming a half circle perimeter around the small group.

"Well played, Jack," laughed the taller, Scottish pirate, as he glanced over, seeing Tobias nod slightly but noticeable enough. With that, both pirates jumped back in unison, swords and dirks drawn and Sofia, seeing this as her cue, stepped forward, next to Tobias, weapons in hand.

Jack grabbed his dagger at his side but before he was able to thrust the knife into Tobias, Sofia threw her dagger and drilled it into Jack's hand, forcing him to drop his dagger and grunt in pain. As if that was the signal for chaos to ensue; bodies, swords, daggers and dirks were flying. Sofia, handling two, sometimes three of Captain Jack's men simultaneously, had the occasional break to glance over at the two pirates who fought back-to-back, handling two to three men themselves. Captain Jack, impressively enough, sparred a bit with some onlookers, who seemed to have an itch for fighting or a distain for him. He was still able to defend himself, although those he fought seemed to simply lose interest in fighting an injured, aging pirate. Tobias neither picked up sword nor dagger nor did he move an inch, as the fighting went on around him, with Sofia drawing the ire of Captain Jack's men. The last of the fighting came to a grinding halt, with the very last man falling dead just inches away from Sofia. The shorter of Tobias' pirates gave Sofia a half-cocked smile, as she spun around on heels just as the Irishman pulled his sword from the dead man's chest.

"At your service, Captain," he exclaimed, with an awkward bow. Sofia looked around surveying the tavern, the only ones still standing were her, Tobias, and his two men. And drinking at the bar was Captain Jack. A slow and steady stream of blood dripping from his hand onto the floorboards, as he drank, while staring at Tobias, who still had not moved a muscle nor wavered his gaze from Captain Jack. Sofia turned her attention to the two men.

"I'm Hugh and this is Benny," said the tall Scot.

"Captain Sofia Bonny Rose, I thank you both for the help!"

"Tobias is a friend of ours and he had a sense there might be some trouble here." said Hugh, glancing back towards Captain Jack.

"Is Tobias alright?" She asked, in awe of the discipline and concentration the man possessed in order to stand as still as a statue, while chaos ensued around him.

"Aye, that he is!" Hugh laughed.

Benny gave a quick smile adding, "Tobias doesn't take kindly to anyone getting in the middle of one of his deals."

"How long does he intend to stand there not moving?"

Benny laughed, realizing how this must look to her but he and Hugh knew Tobias fairly well and they knew Tobias would not move off Captain Jack until the Captain was gone from the tavern.

"Well, I will take my leave but rest assured mister, you haven't heard the last of Captain Jack!" And with that, the fowl-smelling captain turned on heels and walked out the door.

Tobias walked casually over to the man behind the bar and gave him a bag of coins. "This should cover the damage and your trouble for removing the bodies." He went over to Sofia. "Thank you for your assistance and do remember we have a deal." He said, as if none of the past hour had taken place. He motioned for the boys. With that they tipped their hats, as a well-rehearsed duo, and followed Tobias closely out of the tavern. Sofia played the absurdities of the day over in her head, as she exited. Captain Jack was found murdered weeks later, dagger to the heart on Nassau. Although his killer had never been revealed, Sofia couldn't help but think Tobias even more cunning and ruthless than his looks revealed. She liked and trusted him even more after that.

Chapter 11

The next several days were commonplace, daily chores, fair amount of card games and sword play amongst the crew. On their best behavior for all of a day or so, Hugh and Benny were up to their old tricks and some new ones. They hid the cook's ingredients for dinner one day, stole a shirt from one of the younger crew and ran it up the foremast and in general made utter nuisances of themselves.

"We need them, they are notable fighters!" Sofia would repeat over and over to herself after every ruse.

"Sail Ho! Sail Ho! Captain!" Yelled Jessiah from the crow's nest.

Sofia and Mac ran onto the deck. "What flag do you see?" She asked.

"Looks to be a Spanish ship, Captain." Sofia looked at Mac, dawning the look of a Cheshire Cat. She turned and commanded, "Chase!" And with that the crew readied to give chase and board the Spanish ship. Spritely, *The Margola* came upon the Spanish vessel, "Run a shot across the bow!" Sofia ordered. A white flag of surrender was slowly raised aboard the Spanish ship. Sofia stepped confidently over the gangplank, hair tucked into her white painter's shirt and her shirt neatly tucked into a pair of specially made slacks. She was followed closely by Mac, Jessiah and the majority of her crew, all ready for battle, if the need should arise.

"Who is captain of this vessel?" She said, as she placed her right hand on the hilt of her sword, hanging from her waist.

A young black-haired, blue-eyed man, slightly shorter than herself, stepped out in front of Sofia, "I am Mateo Barroso, Captain of the *Sao Mateus*. My crew and I will not fight!"

Sofia flinched slightly in surprise of the quality of the Captain's English. She was instantly attracted to him but possessed the discipline to quell any such feelings. "We'll be taking your cargo, Captain! Have your men gather next to you." she said, showing no signs of weakness.

Captain Barroso looked intently at Sofia; certain he was seeing a woman. But women pirates were so uncommon he'd never heard nor known anyone who came into contact with one.

"*Reunirse a mi lado*!" The young Captain ordered loudly; gaze fixed on Sofia. She didn't know the exact translation but men started gathering around him.

There were no sounds, save the sounds of men moving from various parts of the ship to the center of the deck, the gentle crashing of waves against the ship and the slight movement of the gangplank from the gentle to-and-fro of the water below. Once the Spanish Captain's crew stood before Sofia and her crew, she held up her right hand. At that, Mac led the crew down to the cargo hold, leaving Jessiah, Hugh and Benny to guard Captain Barroso and his men. It wasn't long before Mac and the crew were back on deck carrying gold bars, coins and an assortment of wines and spirits, apparently meant for trade in the colonies. As her crew made their way over the gangplank and back onto *The Margola*, Sofia, Jessiah, Benny and Hugh held their positions, all with their weapons at the ready until the last of their crew had crossed over.

"I thank ye, Captain, for your courtesy. I was not wanting any bloodshed on this day!" With that, she tipped her triangular hat and started walking backwards towards the gangplank.

"We'll be seeing one another again, I'm certain of it." said the Captain, in his best English, with a thick Spanish accent.

"Oh, I look forward to it!" With that Sofia turned and crossed the gangplank, while her men closed ranks around her, slowly backing up in choreographed moves. Once everyone was safely back on board *The Margola* and the gangplank, removed they pulled away from The *Sao Mateus*.

"Well how did we do fellas?" Sofia asked, pleased with herself and the proficiency of which her crew had conducted the thievery. Benny and Hugh had already cracked a bottle open and had just about consumed all of its' contents.

"We have enough to split with the crew and to donate a portion to our friends in Nassau," Mac said, surrounded by the loot. Sofia smiled and nodded in contentment. She turned towards the Spanish ship, now not more than the size of a toy, heading for the horizon. The thought of meeting Captain Barroso again was exhilarating. Thoughts of Captain Barroso were interrupted by loud, dying-cat-like noises coming from two slightly intoxicated pirates. She looked over at Benny and Hugh, who were now swaying to-and-fro, mimicking something sounding like a song, arms around one another.

"Good thing these two are feared for their fighting prowess." she thought, as she walked away, shaking her head and covering her ears.

Sofia made her way down to where the prisoner was held. "Go get something to eat from the cook," she told the boy's guard.

"Yes Captain!" He said eagerly.

The boy was sitting on the floor, arms interlocked around his knees and head down, little waves of sunlight seeping through the cracks danced on his red waves, and from a distance it looked like his head was ablaze. She instantly felt pity for this boy, no more than a child.

"Boy," she called out to him.

He looked up; face stained by free-flowing tears. "Yes, Captain," he croaked, clearing his throat.

"Stand and come over to me!" Sofia commanded, doing her best to suppress any hint of sympathies in her voice. He rose and hobbled the few steps, one leg bound and chained to the back wall. "You didn't tell me all you know. You can have a home with us, and nobody will harm you. But you need to tell me what you're leaving out." Sofia saw a small brand on the boy's hand, something Keen did to prisoners he was selling, so she knew he had no allegiance to him. She stepped back in anticipation of additional surprises.

The boy looked up at Sofia, took in a deep breath, "Keen knows the orb isn't with the treasure at the ship wreck. He knows this, because he heard it is in the hands of a black pirate, named Apollo."

Sofia's heart was beating wildly inside her chest, "Apollo?"

The boy continued, still not letting out his breath, "Word is he went to the wreckage to find the orb. Captain Keen thinks ye know more than he about this Apollo and his current whereabouts. The Captain wants the orb just as much as he wants to see ye dead. He rants about how ye aren't fit to be a pirate, let alone a Captain and ye will soon know your place."

With this he was gasping for air, completely out of breath.

"My place?" Sofia said indignantly. "Why does he want the orb? How does he even know about the orb?"

Red took a deep breath, as if he were going to swim minutes underwater, "Ye see this old witch in Barbados told him about the orb that sank. It has magical powers of clues to future happenings." He let out the rest of his breath, as he finished with surprising brevity.

Sofia momentarily forgot about the ridiculous comments about her role Black Heart uttered to Red and focused on the witch in Barbados, her witch. Why would the woman tell her and Black Heart about the orb and *The Capitana Mia*?

Chapter 12

A blanket of grey mist covered from the tops of the water to the top of the crow's nest, as far as the eye could see. A hazy cloud moving to the natural rhythm of the ship. The crew sang and hummed, while tending to the daily affairs of the ship. Red, the would-be spy, had warned them Captain Keen's plan of attack was to take place close to land, off the island of Barbados. Since they had not yet crossed into Trinidad and Tobago's waters just south of Barbados, they still had time to prepare.

Jessiah slowly climbed upwards to the crow's nest platform to relieve his fellow crew of his watch.

Although he enjoyed the banter and companionship of his crew mates, there was nothing better than his quiet throne, high above the waves. A silhouette in the distance caught his eye through the fog.

"Ships!" the word escaped from his mouth as a screeching howl, as he hurried his climb.

Some crew stopped in their wake, unsure what they heard, while others kept about their business. Jessiah moved with cat-like reflexes up to the nest but just as he stepped onto the nest's deck, earth-shattering crashes sandwiched *The Margola* into a death's trap, sending Jessiah off the side of the platform, clinging to the rope ladder.

Without warning, planks flung down on both sides of the trapped ship and menacing men of various shapes and sizes armed with swords and guns flooded *The Margola*'s deck, leaving little time for the stunned crew to mass a credible defense. Within minutes, clangs of swords and the occasional blast broke through the silence of the surreal scene taking place on *The Margola*'s deck. The second ship, hitting starboard side, seemed to have one purpose, to isolate and kidnap *The Margola*'s captain. Pirates marched in teams, ignoring the chaos of the ship's crew fighting off the Portside attackers and zeroing in on one tall, brown-haired captain. Sofia positioned herself in between the wheel and wall of her cabin, stabbing one pirate assailant after another, as if they were contestants in line taking turns to dethrone the current champion.

"Enough!" Thundered a stout black-bearded man, "All of you, go and take her!" He pointed to several men standing just feet from him. At that directive, the men descended upon her, swords clutched capably in their hands.

"No!" Cried Benny, glancing across the deck, both he and Hugh busy clashing swords and dirks with several foul-smelling pirates themselves. Sofia was able to take a deep breath as the contestants quickly shifted out of the way for the pirate party of six to cut into the seemingly endless dance. Her hair now flowing, and shirt completely untucked from her pants, she readied for a battle, having no intention to lose. The pirates surrounded her, as she thrashed about with sword in one hand and dirk in the other, both working independently yet in complete concert with one another. Two of the taller pirates ran at her but she cut them down with fierce precision, as the remaining four nodded to one another and charged at her, two having swords drawn in hand and the other two armed with dirks held at their sides. Sofia swung dirk and sword violently, eyes shifting from one assailant to another but was unable to emerge beyond the defense position. As she was lured slightly starboard, one of the pirate assailants seized the moment and delivered a thunderous blow to the back of Sofia's head. Lacking theatrics, she reflexively dropped her weapons and gracefully fell to the deck, as Keen's henchmen quickly carried her limp body over the gangplank onto Keen's ship.

Chapter 13

Sofia blinked several times, eyes diligently working to focus through the throbbing pain streaking through her head. She moved slightly, rattling the metal chains at her wrists, giving her just enough slack to touch the back of her head. Through her thick, wavy hair, she felt the large, swollen bump, wet and sticky from her blood, slowly oozing. It all came rushing back, she remembered and instantly knew whose watery prison she was an unwilling guest. She giggled slightly to herself, finding the irony in her unfortunate current circumstance. All the times she'd been able to outrun, outfight and outsmart Captain Tyberias "Black Heart" Keen and he gets the better of her with the involuntary actions of a child. She started to giggle to herself again when that train of thought was replaced by panic.

"Mac! The boys!" She said out loud. She closed her eyes and searched her memory for the last few minutes before she blacked out. Every thought, every recollection seemed jumbled and convoluted at the moment, with images coming in and out. She opened her eyes, looking for ideas of escape, looking for something within reach to help loosen the binding holding the chains to the floor restraining her ability to kill Captain Black Heart. Surges of adrenaline coursed through her veins, like a live electrical wire, as she traversed from prisoner to huntress.

❈ ❈ ❈

Blood flowing from a dirk to the side, Mac hobbled to the foremast, now fully ablaze.

"Mac, are you harmed?" Jessiah asked, before seeing the trail of blood. Without uttering another word, he pulled his own shirt up over his head, ripped the bottom into several strips and expertly wrapped them securely around Mac's middle. "That should do to stem the bleeding," He said breathlessly.

Paying no attention to his wound or the new accessory to his middle, "Get that fire out!" Mac yelled.

Several crew members who weren't injured or killed were already working on extinguishing or, at the very least, containment. Mac was briskly moving about the ship, looking for Hugh and Benny, as he knew they were fighting closely to Sofia. The two men were triaging the wounded, mending dislocated shoulders and stuffing strips of cloth into bleeding wounds.

"Where's Sofia?" Mac asked, with desperation noticeable in his voice.

The two men looked at one another and Mac knew, Keen had her. "We tried to get to her Mac! We tried but we each had two men on us and we couldn't reach her before Keen's men knocked her on the head and dragged her off." Hugh looked over at Benny, head down in despair, then quickly glanced at Mac, visibly shaken.

Mac nodded slowly. "Tend to the men," he ordered softly.

The fire was out, and the mast burnt beyond use but they still had two sails, strong and capable, allowing them to make the rest of the way to Nassau. He felt a pit in the middle of his stomach, as thoughts of Sofia in the clutches of Black Heart came over him like a tidal wave. One on one, he had little qualms of Sofia coming out the victor but knocking her out meant she was surely stripped of her weapons and bound. While he didn't know Keen's full intentions, he knew the plan would not include her coming back to her ship.

❀ ❀ ❀

Sofia felt a presence near her, watching her, "Come out and face me!" Sofia ordered indignantly. Red slowly stepped out of the shadows and into the dimly-lit space in front of her but out of Sofia's grasp. Her rage-filled gaze forced Red's eyes to cower downward as he stepped back another two steps, as if she was suddenly able to break her chains and ring his neck. Not only could she feel her heart beating rapidly, but she could also hear it as it pounded louder and louder, taking over her every fiber of her being. She was starting to feel faint, blood seemingly flowing away from her head, and blood vessels widening.

"Captain, are ye ok?" asked Red.

Sofia, now head down between her knees, taking deeper, longer breaths, as her heartbeat started slowing. Blood was flowing back to her head and with it an increased pain.

"What do you want?" She growled, breathlessly.

"I never had the intention to see ye harmed. Believe me, I did not know what I overheard was the trap itself!" He said, with tears welling up in the corner of his eyes. "I aim to make this right!" He pronounced vigorously.

She lifted her head, hearing faint sounds and sensing she was about to have a visit from her host. "Hide now!" Sofia urged, as she heard the rhythmic movements of multiple boots reverberating on the ship's wooden steps. Red obeyed, slipping behind some crates. She took another deep breath, gathering her wits about her.

※ ※ ※

"Why, if it isn't Sofia Bonny Rose, ya seem to be all tied up at the moment, Ms. Rose." Keen let out a maniacal laugh, clearly amusing himself. He abruptly stopped in mid-laugh, catching and holding Sofia's gaze; the ferocity of it sending a slight shiver down his spine. Her breathing controlled, showing little signs of distress, ready for the cat-and-mouse games to begin. Seeing her lack of concern and prolonged silence was slowly driving him mad, as she maintained eye contact, knowing it would force him to the make the first move.

"You've nothing to say on the day of yer death?"

"It's not me who will be doing the dying." She responded, casually and confidently. Just as she repositioned herself, he lunged at her, grabbed her by the back of her hair and pulled down, hard.

"Ya won't be so cock sure of yourself for long!" He pulled her hair downward again, forcing a small noise from her, then let go, stepping back so she was forced to see all of him. She worked to slow her breathing, part of what she did to collect herself.

"I can't kill ya outright, I will lose respect with my men, so I challenge ya to a duel by pistols."

Sofia's eyes narrowed as she fixed a death gaze onto him, "Challenge me to a duel by swords!" She demanded, with hands reflexively balled up into fists, as she pulled at the chains that bound her.

He snorted forcefully, "Do ya think I'm so stupid I would place a sword in your hand? Ha! I'm not fool enough to think I am a better swordsman than ya. I've seen ya fight, I've fought ya. And ya can beat every man I have."

Somewhat taken aback by the compliment, she opened her fists, "Well at least we agree on one thing," she said, mildly sarcastic. "What makes you think I can't dislodge a shot faster and with more accuracy than you?"

"Ha!" He let out a strangled sort of noise, sounding something like a laugh. "I don't plan on giving ya a loaded weapon. This is just for looks, so I can rid myself of ya once and for all."

Sofia nodded slightly, digesting the plan and feeling a little sullen he was ending their long-running cat-and-mouse game. The realization suddenly hit her, she needed to buy herself additional time for Mac and *The Margola* to come for her.

"Pretty good plan!" She admitted, "You guarantee yourself the victor, while saving face with your crew."

"It's quite the ingenious plan, if I do say so myself." He admitted, lacking any hint of humility.

"It is that. I'm rather impressed you thought of such a plan all by yourself." She said smiling. Keen looked at her intently, sensing she was toying with him but he was enjoying their usual game and banter.

He was going to miss the challenge, he thought to himself, as they once again locked eyes but her skills with the sword was becoming more refined and he could no longer take the chance of her gaining the upper hand on him.

Chapter 14

Blood was seeping through Mac's make-shift bandage, as he slowly made his way checking on crew, making note on who was killed and who was wounded.

"We need to mend that properly," warned Jessiah, surveying the amount of blood soaking through his patch work. Much to his surprise, Mac didn't argue. He nodded in exhaustion and leaned back, resting on a sack. Jessiah spent some time learning healing from a doctor. He had a healthy number of herbs to help headaches and small wounds, but he excelled at tailoring. To look at him, slightly disheveled and never particularly tidy, one would never guess him somewhat of a master organizer. Mac wasn't much surprised to see Jessiah thumbing through a box filled with herbs, pulling out a needle and thread, along with a bottle of alcohol for sterilization. Mac started laughing nervously, having never actually seen Jessiah sew anything, let alone his skin together.

"Not to worry, I've seen this done many times!" He chuckled, before turning to see his patient less then amused and looking rather like he was going to be ill. "Aye, I'm joking I've, indeed, sewn many a man, with the good doctor, of course."

Mac gave a weak attempt at a smile, "Let's get on with it." He grabbed the bottle of whiskey and drank a healthy amount to dull the pain.

"It's a wicked gash and you'll have a long, healthy scar but I think this should do," Mac said, tying the final knot in the string. Mac looked down at Jessiah's handy work.

Jessiah grabbed the bottle from Mac's hand, poured a little alcohol next to the stitching, then gently wiped the blood off around it.

"Fine work, Jessiah, I thank you!"

Jessiah smiled. He quickly packed up his healing box, "You rest yourself a while, I'm going to help Hugh and Benny with the others."

He was gone before Mac could respond. Mac smiled at the thought of Hugh and Benny. He hadn't wanted them on board but now he was grateful they were there, and no one could argue their loyalty to

Sofia. Their skills and swordsmanship had come in handy but more so now was his familiarity with them and knowing they would stop at nothing to help get Sofia back. Keen had found their weakness – numbers. Sofia ran a small crew, which was both their strength and their weakness. Keen finally figured it out. He didn't have to have the best or the fiercest, he just needed more of them.

Mac fell asleep where he lay, propped on top of a sack, head leaning back against the side of the ship. He was drifting, lost to a state of diminished consciousness, floating above *The Margola* in search of The *Black Revenge*, Keen's ship. Images of Sofia, Keen, the red-headed traitor, the wounded and dead crew all flashed before him, creating surges of anger moving through his muscles like a marionette controlled by strings. He awoke to beams of sun shining down, covered in sweat from nightmarish images and wicked pains from his wound. He lay there for a moment, recalling some of the less intensely disturbing images to an image based on Sofia's description of the Pirate Apollo. He went to jump up, only remembering he was wounded when multiple arrows of pain shot through his middle. Slumping back down on top of the sack, he took a deep breath, slowly let it out and carefully pulled himself upright. "Better." he thought to himself, as he went back focusing on finding Hugh and Benny.

The wounded were laid systematically, two-by-two, on the deck below, allowing for their caregivers to easily traverse between one patient and another. Mac stepped lightly down the makeshift aisle, feeling responsible for each and every one of the souls laying injured before him. At the end of one of the aisles, Hugh and Benny laid on the floor, looking as if they'd been dropped where they stood. Asleep, from sheer exhaustion.

"Guys! Wake up, wake up!" Mac went from a sort of whisper to a not-so-gradual howl.

"What?" Benny, usually the more reserved of the two growled, startling Mac by grabbing his arm, with his eyes still closed.

Mac pulled back. "Let go of me...listen, we need to find Apollo!"

At the mention of Apollo, both Benny and Hugh opened their eyes, showing signs of life. "Apollo?" Asked the two men simultaneously.

"Yes, Apollo, your Captain!" Bellowed Mac, a hint of frustration in his voice. "Look, we need help, half of our men are either dead or wounded and there is a connection with him and Sofia, right?" His voice trembled through the hurried words.

"Aye," the two resigned, once again in harmonic-styling unison.

"If he's out on the open ocean, he could be anywhere. Our only hope is back on the island." said Hugh.

"The island? Barbados! Right?" Mac didn't wait for an answer but moved as quickly as he found physically possible to find Jessiah.

Back on the main deck, feeling the effects of his wound and general fatigue, he stood in the middle and yelled as loud as he was able, "Jessiah!"

"I'm here Mac, is it your wound, did the stitches pull out."

"No, we need to head back to Barbados, now!"

"Barbados? Whatever for…what about Sofia?"

Mac winced and grabbed his side, taking a much-needed breath, "We need to find Apollo, we can't do anything for Sofia like this."

At that, Jessiah didn't wait for any further explanation but ran about waking up whatever crew were fit enough to work, changing course to Barbados. They weren't far from the island and within minutes, *The Margola* had course-corrected for Barbados.

Chapter 15

The Margola pulled into Barbados well after nightfall. Mac left Jessiah in charge of the crew and maintenance of the ship while he, Hugh and Benny searched for Apollo. The town was a haven for pirates, privateers, the convicted and the condemned. Smells of rum permeated the streets as the stench of grime and filth from its' guests wafted in the air, at the pleasure of the gentle breeze. Some structures were illuminated by lanterns, while others stood dark as the night around them. They tried several of Apollo's usual haunts and subtly asked around but no word of him.

"People on this island are very loyal to Apollo, so they won't tell of his whereabouts unless they have his blessing." Informed Benny.

"Why in the world are they loyal to him? He's a pirate!" Inquired Mac, a little taken aback by hearing how one of his own could possibly achieve such ardent loyalty and support from a people. Pirates were always considered outcasts, dregs of society, thugs and thieves.

"Aye but Apollo is a different type of pirate. On the sea, he is as ruthless or worse than the rest but on land he gives to the citizens of this island. He gives them money and hope in hard times. So, to them, he is only a good man!"

Mac gave a rueful smile, thinking about the pirates and privateers he'd known, the selfish acts of plundering benefiting no other souls than themselves. Then, he thought back to Sofia and how frustrated he was the first time they "came" into money, watching as she dispersed a good sum to him and the rest to the crew but keeping a nice portion for those downtrodden. He and the rest of the crew became accustomed to her holding back on them because she convinced them they would need to rely on the kindness of these same folks one day. For the first time, he understood and that made him more determined to find Apollo and rescue Sofia.

"This way, sometimes he takes a room at The Inn," said Hugh, leading them down a dark corridor to a plain-looking door. Inside, there were tables scattered about, some men seated and others standing by the bar drinking and talking. It was quieter and less inhabited than the other establishments they'd visited since arriving on the island.

"This is a place known for conducting business," said Hugh. "There are no women allowed and at the first sign of trouble the proprietor has a reputation for tossing folks."

"I think she's even killed one or two!" Added Benny casually.

Mac's eyes widened at hearing the proprietor was a woman. "A woman, you say, and she doesn't allow women in?"

"Aye! She knows the distractions women bring and does not want her place known for that." Explained Benny.

Hugh stopped in the middle of the room, squinting to see what appeared as a small-framed shape on the other side, at a little table where the light couldn't reach. "Awe, she's there!" He said, triumphantly.

Mac and Benny followed him to the little table, where the small-framed shape sat.

"We need to find Apollo, is he here?" asked Hugh.

"Why are you here and without The Pirate Queen, I see?" Commentary riddled with sarcasm from the mysterious figure. Mac's ears perked up, looking from the figure, to eyes shifting upstairs, then back to the figure. His eyes narrowed at the one sitting in front of him and a large piece to the puzzle revealed.

"It's you!" He said, aghast.

The woman looked up, pulled the cloak's hood down, revealing herself. "It's who?" She demanded, her voice deep and unsettling.

"You're Sofia's witch!" He stumbled over the words and did his best to keep his voice low, as to not attract any further attention.

The woman smirked, eyes smiling, "If you mean I am the one who told her of *The Capitana Mia* then, yes, I am her witch, as you say."

"I mean you no disrespect." added Mac.

Before he was able to continue along that thought, she made a motion with her hand, ending the conversation. "Upstairs, the last room in the center of the hall." She said, looking at Hugh. "He will not be pleased you are here!" She warned.

Mac opened his mouth to speak again but Hugh pushed him slightly, as a warning to stop, while they could. They made their way up the stairs and to the room the witch directed them to. The door opened slightly, revealing part of a familiar face.

"Ishmael, it's us! We need to see him right away."

"Who is us?" Asked Ishmael, the sarcasm notable in his voice.

Before Hugh was able to answer, he heard a voice sternly command, "Let them in Ishmael!" With that, the door was opened just wide enough and long enough for the three men to walk into the room, then promptly shut behind them.

"Why are you here?" asked Apollo, standing, revealing his true size.

Mac quickly stepped in front of Hugh, "Keen has Sofia!"

Apollo's eyes narrowed and directed a menacing gaze at Hugh, then Benny and back to Hugh, fists clenched in disapproval.

Seeing this, Mac spoke up on their behalf. "They are not to blame for this! Keen ambushed us with two ships, we took a fair amount of casualties and damage to *The Margola*. Your men fought bravely!" Said Mac, turning to catch the gaze of both men giving him a nod of thanks.

Apollo softened, nodded to Ishmael who, at that, slipped out of the room. "We will take my ship, The *Redemption*, at first light." Said Apollo, with a commanding voice.

"The witch downstairs, the owner of this establishment, who is she and how does she know Sofia? She told Sofia about The *Capitana Mia* but *you* have the orb…"

"Is there a question in that sir?" Asked Apollo, cutting Mac's list of seemingly rambling statements.

Mac regrouped, took a deep breath, "What's the witch's connection to Sofia and what's your connection to the witch?" Asked Mac.

The creases of Apollo's mouth turned up slightly, "Awe, but that's not the correct question, now is it?" Said Apollo, now toying with Mac. "The better question is how is everyone related to the orb and what is Sofia's place in this?" He laughed at that, then pursed his lips, "Let's get the girl back first, then we will find the answers!" His voice was stern and unwavering. He held his hand up, signaling it was time for the men to go and with that Hugh grabbed Mac by the sleeve of his shirt and prodded him out the door. The three men headed back downstairs in silence. Mac, visibly showing his frustration, made his way over to the table in the shadows, where the witch had sat. She was gone and not a sight of her anywhere.

"You won't find her, if she doesn't want to be found." Benny informed Mac.

"What do you two know about all this?" He asked.

"Listen, Mac," Hugh sighed, heavily, "only Apollo can answer the questions you have. We need to get her back first."

Mac nodded in agreement, refocusing his attention on finding and rescuing Sofia.

Chapter 16

At first light, Mac, Hugh and Benny were already standing at the foot of the gangplank, waiting Apollo's arrival and direction. The black pirate was known for ghost-like movements, rarely spotted in public, so it was of no surprise to the three men to hear the creaking sounds of the wood plank behind them. Apollo boarded the *Redemption*, followed closely by Ishmael.

"How…" Mac started asking but quickly shook his head and closed his mouth, as the men made their way up the gangplank. The *Redemption*'s deck didn't look all that dissimilar from *The Margola*, although The *Redemption* was a slightly larger ship, and her crew were twice the number of *The Margola*.

"The three of you follow me!" Directed Apollo, leading the men to his quarters. The room, surprisingly modest, possessing a bed, several chairs, a number of maps and charts adorning the walls. But Mac was drawn to the table in the middle of the room. It was sizable, for the room, and round. In every ship he'd been on, including *The Margola*, the tables had been rectangular in shape.

Apollo caught sight of Mac and walked over to the table. "I wanted a place for my top people to feel a shared power, a shared vision."

Mac looked up from admiring the table and smiled, nodding, realizing this was no usual captain and no usual man.

"You see," Apollo continued, "My men know I am in command!" He laughed, thinking about it, "I have earned my reputation in battle, on the seas, so I don't need to on my ship!"

Mac nodded in agreement, with a new-found respect for the mysterious Captain.

Apollo pulled a couple of maps from the wall and laid them on the round table, "Sit, please" he motioned the men towards the chairs. "Now…" started the Captain, clearing his throat, "We know Keen has an obsession with Sofia, we know he's tried many times to kill her…"

"We know she's shown him a fool in front of his men." interrupted Mac, taking a deep breath.

"He's going to kill her in front of his men on the ship." Apollo concluded and Mac nodded in solemn agreement.

"She's a far better swordsman!" Said Hugh, getting to his feet, pacing the length of the room.

"Aye, but he doesn't fight fair, now does he?" Added Benny.

The men stood and sat in silence, until Apollo rose from the table and went over to a little cabinet. He pulled out a bottle of rum, took a hard drink straight from the bottle and passed it on to Mac.

After propelling through the sea for only a few hours, thanks to winds in their favor, the door to the cabin opened. "Captain, the ship's been spotted," said Ishmael, calmly.

"Is it The *Black Revenge*?" Asked Apollo, not turning around.

"We believe it is Captain!"

Apollo nodded, "Have everyone ready for battle!" His voice calm yet commanding.

"Aye Captain," Ishmael hurried out of the room.

Apollo turned and nodded to Hugh and with that the four men exited the cabin and loaded themselves with gun powder and extra daggers.

❈ ❈ ❈

Left alone in total darkness, with only thoughts of the morning, Sofia pushed back against the wall and closed her eyes allowing the gentle rocking of the waves to take her into a temporary void. She awoke in darkness, hearing light footsteps coming down to the hold.

"Who's there?" She asked softly, as to not awaken more of the deplorable element that was Keen's crew.

"It's Alex," a young Scottish voice whispered.

"Red?" She asked, a little surprised.

"Aye Captain, it's me," he said breathlessly, making his way over to her.

"What are you doing here? You're going to get yourself killed!" She pushed herself to her knees and leaned back, focusing her eyes to see his slim shape come into view.

He knelt beside her. "Take it," he said, guiding her hand to the handle of a dirk. "Hide it, they will'na search ye because they already took your weapons. I can't get you a sword without being found." He said, with a confidence she hadn't seen before.

"Thank You!" She whispered, "Now, go before you get discovered!" She caressed the hilt of the Scottish dirk in her palm, as she watched his shadow disappear into the blackness. She gripped the hilt hard, sat back down, leaned back against the wall and placed the weapon gently in her boot.

It wasn't too long before light started creeping down the stairs, ever so delicately at first, then an energetic explosion devouring the shadows. Sofia heard voices, and the pounding of feet from above. She moved to her knees; eyes fixed on the stairs. There were several sets of footsteps coming down towards Sofia and from the amount of daylight, she knew they were coming for her. A surprising calm came over her, but having the dirk gave her strength and focus, as she waited to reclaim control of her fate. Several male figures walked quickly towards her. After they had gathered before her, she counted seven of them. It figures, she thought to herself, Keen was too afraid I could overpower a couple of his men.

One of the men lunged at her, grabbing her by the throat. "You killed a friend of mine!" He growled, "I'll be all too happy to see ye die like the swine ye are!" He let go of his grip and pushed her back, then she rocked to one side, still on her knees, reclaimed her balance with clenched fists and narrowed her gaze at the lot in front of her.

She smirked, "I only kill those deserving to be killed!"

He spun around on his heels at hearing her comment, arms outstretched in a fit of rage.

One of the other men grabbed his wrist, "Stop this, the Captain will deal with her!" he said, with the slight foreign accent Sofia recognized as Italian.

The attacker stared at Sofia, let out a couple of heavy grunts and walked back through the hold. The man who stopped the attack leered for what seemed like forever to her, then directed the remainder of the men to step back and keep watch, while he unhooked the prisoner. Sofia held steady, impenetrable gaze fixed on the man approaching her, as he knelt down back to the men.

"There's gun powder in this," he whispered, while slowly unlocking the shackles. She grabbed the small leather bag with her unlocked hand and quickly placed it in her boot.

"Why are you helping me?" She whispered.

"I owe ya my life, now hush and pull and moan!"

She gave a slight nod, yelling. "Get off of me! Let me go!" As he unlocked the other hand, forced her hands together and shackled them together. She was still on her knees when he motioned for the men.

"Stand her up and take her up to the deck. She's a strong one, don't let her get the better of you!" He barked.

Two of the men surrounded her, seizing her arms, pushing her forwards, while the others followed closely behind. The man stood watching until he heard the last of the footsteps pounding the stairs.

"Red, get out here!" He barked. The young Scot sheepishly emerged from his favorite hiding place behind an old stack of crates. The man, dark in features, 5'10", a solid build, and in his latter 20's, grabbed the boy by his shirt and pulled him within inches of his face. "What do you think you're doing?

Do you know what will happen to you if Keen finds out you've been down here?" He snapped.

"I…owe her, sir" stuttered the boy, barely audible.

The man let go with a nod, "As do I," he said ruefully, "What did you give her?"

"Nothing!" Red objected, "I did'na give her a thing!"

The man glared at Red, "You're not in trouble, I need to know so we can help her not get killed." he explained, in a whisper.

Red sighed audibly, "A dirk, but Marco, I couldn't get to a sword."

The creases of Marco's wide mouth turned up, "It's all right, I gave her some powder for the empty gun Keen plans to give her."

"Empty gun?" Asked Red, shaking his head.

"Aye, how do you think he plans to kill her. He knows he doesn't have a chance with her. You've seen her fight."

Red nodded slowly in agreement, still processing how low Captain Keen would go to win.

Marco was instantly taken with Red and quickly became his protector, after he was forced on the ship. He was the reason Red was still on the *Black Revenge,* instead of sold off into servitude on some island. "Go hide yourself and I swear to you, if I see you up on deck, I'll kill ya myself! *Capisci?*"

Red nodded, hearing Marco speak enough in his native tongue to know he was asking if he understood. Red turned back towards his crates and Marco made his way up the stairs, readying for the dramatics.

Chapter 17

Sofia's escorts affixed her chains around one of the masts in the center of the deck. She didn't fight it, conserving her strength for what was coming next. The crew started assembling, forming a large perimeter around Sofia. Captain Keen made his way onto the deck in ceremonial fashion, men cheered, chanting, "Kill her!" as he strutted towards her. A short, rotund fellow hastened behind, carrying a box.

"Awe, well I thank ye kindly for joining me on this day o' your death, Ms. Rose. It's going to be a bang…ha, ha, ha."

Sofia couldn't help but roll her eyes, "The least you could do is to make a witty joke before we begin." She said a bit annoyed.

Keen leaned in within inches of her face, "I'll be getting the last laugh, as I send ya to hell!"

"Your stench is going to kill me before the pistol, if you don't get out of my face!" She hissed, through gritted teeth.

He lunged forward and licked her cheek, as she squirmed and moaned in disgust, "Now ye have my stench on ya for eternity!"

The thought of that, along with the smell, made Sofia want to gag right there. Before stepping back, Keen grabbed the dagger hanging on his hip and sliced her other cheek, "Best not to turn the other cheek now!" He said.

Sofia let out a small noise and turned back with such intensity and fierceness in her eyes it made Keen step back even further.

"I will kill you!" She said, with a remarkable amount of calm. He slowly turned his head away from her, mouth slightly open in stupefaction and summoned the short, rotund fellow with the wooden box. The man opened the box, revealing two pistols. After what looked to be some thought at which to choose, Black Heart grabbed the pistol laying on the left side. Without saying a word, he pointed to Sofia and the man scurried over to her and laid the remaining weapon at her feet, then promptly backed away, as if she could magically remove the chains and cause him harm. Black Heart turned on heel and walked down several feet, while turning to face Sofia, and waving his hand in the air in an obvious signal the main event was underway.

Several men surrounded her, one unshackling her from the mast and two others who grabbed her arms before she was able to make any attempt at moving.

Marco appeared in front of her, raising the pistol and holding it out over his two hands for her. "I trust you will be honorable."

Sofia gave a slight nod and the men let her go and took their positions back amongst the rank and file. She took the pistol, staring at him, and unsure how to get to the gun powder in her boot. The corners of his mouth turned up slightly and he spun around.

"Captain, please permit me to say a prayer over the condemned."

"Aye, fine, but then ye must say a prayer over me as well."

"Certainly." he said.

"Get on your knees." He whispered, turning back to Sofia. She quickly complied, hands appearing together, as if she were truly engaged in a spiritual moment. Marco bent over her, shielding her from their audience, allowing just enough time for Sofia to grab the bag of gun powder and ready the weapon. "The Father, the Son and the Holy Spirit, Amen!" He said, audible enough to make it seem genuine.

"Amen" said Sofia and "Thank you…" she whispered.

Marco walked over to his Captain, who was already kneeling and said a real prayer.

Black Heart rose. "Mr. Mancini, do the honors."

Marco took his place on the side, in-between Black Heart and Sofia, "You will fire on the count of 3…1, 2—"

Before Marco could say the number 3, a thundering reverberation shook the ship, jolting those on board. Another thunderous vibration and another, each one more tumultuous than the previous, causing the ship to violently convulse. The men scattered to their battle-ready stations. Black Heart fired in Sofia's direction but in all the chaos she was able to evade her "handlers" and reach the side of the ship, expecting to see *The Margola*.

"Who in the bloody hell..." Engrossed on who's ship was about to board The *Black Revenge*, few ever dared, she didn't notice the three men who snuck up behind her. She stopped, suddenly feeling the nauseating sensation of hot breath on her neck, and with the dirk Red had slipped her, clutched in her hand, she went to spin around but was met with a hard blow to her head. She fell to her knees, having the presence of mind to slip the dirk back into her boot before the men seized her hands, dragging her back to the mast she was tied to only a short time before. She leaned back, head throbbing, sensing someone's gaze upon her, she straightened up as much as she could, seeing Black Heart pointing a gun at her head.

"You can't do it like this, Captain," she said, breathing heavily. "What will your men think of you, killing me, chained, unable to face me in a fair fight!" She was calm but still breathing hard, head pounding in between words.

Black Heart hesitated, giving some thought to her argument against her execution. Before he was able to render a verdict on her plea, a wide plank crashed down on the *Black Revenge* and a flurry of men, swords, guns and shouting came with it. He turned, momentarily forgetting Sofia and rushing to fend off those suicidal enough to board his ship.

Sofia breathed a sigh of relief as she tried freeing herself from the shackles.

"Stop moving!" A familiar voice said, sternly.

"Red? What in the devil are you doing up here?" She uttered, through clenched teeth.

"Getting you out of these!" His hands were shaking, as he worked the key into the lock.

She took a deep breath, thankful he was there, even though she had ordered him to stay hidden below. She heard a click and the chains slipped off. Red caught them and gently placed them on the floor, hoping everyone was busy fending off the intruding ship to notice Sofia gone but also not to notice him on deck at all.

"This way!" Red whispered, handing Sofia the gun Keen had given her before she was attacked. "How?" She asked, shaking her head, still reeling from the blow.

"It fell to the deck when they attacked ye; I'm ver'a good at not bein' seen." Red was talking at lightning speed, jumbling words in his thick Scottish accent.

"You're quite the thief." She concluded, smiling and motioning him to lead on. She was too large of a presence to hide and Red had the sense to realize Captain Sofia Bonny Rose would never submit to hiding, while a battle was raging all around her. He was leading her to part of the ship, where she could have a better view of the deck, so she wouldn't be in position to have anyone sneak up on her again. Following Red's lead in crouching down, she craned her long neck, surveilling much of the large deck.

"Mac!" She whispered, the corners of her mouth ticking up widely, unable to suppress her excitement and relief. Not too far from him, she spotted Jessiah and there in the middle of the deck, not believing her eyes, stood The Black Ghost himself. "Apollo" she cried out.

"Sh…" Red admonished, "They want ye dead, please, until ye have a plan, keep still and quiet!"

Sofia turned, conceding and nodding in admiration at this young, emboldened version of the boy she had first met on *The Margola*. "I need a sword! Do you think you can get me one?"

Red nodded.

"Without getting yourself killed!" She added.

"Aye, I can!" His eyes, as mischievous as the smirk on his face. She watched, as Mac and Jessiah fought back-to-back, yearning to join them.

It wasn't long before Red came back with a sword, "It's a bonny one!" He said proudly.

Sofia grabbed the sword, caressing it in her palm, as she so often did with hers, feeling every groove and curvature. "You, stay out of sight. I'll come back for you!" She was resolute on bringing him back to *The Margola*. He nodded and ducked down, as she made her way into the thick of the scrum. She knelt down, grabbing the dirk from her boot, placed it in her left hand and, feeling very much like the warrior, she ran towards the ensuing battle.

"Good to see ye Captain," Hugh uttered breathlessly, seeing Sofia locking swords with two of Keen's men.

"What took you guys so long?" She quipped back. Benny gave a loud snort, shaking his head, as he pushed one of Black Heart's men off of him.

"You have no idea the lengths we went through to get to you!" Mac yelled, breathlessly, pausing for a moment, then adding, "You're lucky ya aren't dead!"

She cracked a smile, retorting, "If you had taken any longer, I might have been!" It was as if her own words triggered something inside her and a surge of energy went through her like a lightning bolt, as she whipped the sword around, striking both Benny's attackers dead. She stood there, breathing heavily, dripping adrenaline and sweat, as she turned, eyes searching for one Captain Tyberias "Black Heart" Keen. Black Heart had managed to refrain from the unwanted attention, as he stood away from the epicenter of the fighting. He had struck down three of Sofia's men, waiting for her, taunting her to come at him, as their bodies lay in small pools of blood.

She spotted him from across the deck, taking long, powerful strides sword clutched firmly in her hand and dirk in the other. Mac caught sight of her, finished off one of Black Heart's men and ran towards her.

"No, leave her be! This is her fight alone." Apollo stood, preventing Mac from moving further towards his captain. Mac held up his hand and nodded, signifying to Apollo he understood and wouldn't interfere. Sofia stopped in front of her men lying dead on the deck, she bowed her head in honor of their memory and whispered a vow to avenge their deaths. "We finish this, no tricks, just you and me!" She said, gazing at Black Heart, voice calm and resolute.

"Aye, if ya think I'm going to let ya destroy a lifetime of my reputation, as most feared on the seas, you've another thing comin'!" he roared.

Black Heart's crew gathered nearest to him while Apollo's crew, including Hugh, Benny and Mac, gathered opposite of them. It was as though a magical spell had been cast, freezing everyone where they stood. The two captains stood like prize fighters in the ring, sizing up one another, preparing for battle.

"Come on! Come on old man, you has-been of a pirate!" Sofia taunted, hoping to provoke him and use his anger against him. Black Heart grunted in response, eyeing her, rage building up inside him. "Your men know you're terrified of me! Your men know I'm better with a sword than you are!" She laughed, sensing the tipping point was coming, when he was going to boil over and lunge at her. She took a step towards him, using sword and dirk as extensions of her arms to continue provoking him. There it was, he screamed something incomprehensible, sword flying wildly. Sofia jumped back, eyes sparkling, knowing she had the upper hand, as Black Heart was enraged and making foolish moves. She blocked the first couple of blows with her sword, remembering just how strong he could be, especially when filled with rage. Like a dancer, her moves were graceful, fluid, she was light on her feet, choreographing the finale of a long-running play. Matching sword, stroke-by-stroke, then moving to throw him off balance, she knew all too well she controlled pace and tempo. A low grumble slowly became a rolling roar of cheers, boos and random shouts of curse words and calls for death. Black Heart was starting to slow, he was breathing harder and harder, slightly staggering when something flew in the air. He caught it as he dropped and kicked his sword away. "Let me see ya dodge—" Before Black Heart was able to finish his sentence and fire the pistol, Sofia shoved her sword into his chest striking his black heart. He gasped for air, dropping the gun and clutching at the sword before collapsing in a pool of his blood. Apollo and his men readied for all-out war with the crew, just as Marco stood on a crate, addressing the crew, "Men of The *Black Revenge* today we suffered a great loss, the loss of our leader, Captain Tyberias "Black Heart" Keen. As his second, I am now captain of The *Black Revenge*. If any man takes issue with it, speak now or not again!"

Shock swept through the crew and some relief Black Heart was gone, as not one protest of the new self-appointed captain, just stares at the woman who removed their captain from Earth. "All right then…" Marco said, nodding.

Sofia stood over Black Heart's lifeless body, unable to look away from the man who taunted her for so long. A mixing of emotions swirled inside of her, not knowing if she was relieved, pleased, sorrowful or completely disoriented this constant foe was now, and forevermore, simply gone from this world. Mac, Hugh and Benny stayed back but Apollo moved beside her.

"You have the orb, I want it!" She said, not taking her eyes off of the body.

"I do, I found The *Capitana Mia* and the orb where it's rested for years." Apollo said, taking a step closer to her.

"What's my connection to it? What does it have to do with my parents?" She was whispering now, acutely aware of all the eyes resting upon her and Apollo.

"Listen child, you are a part of a special group of people. Your parents asked I watch over you in the event something should happen to them. You are where you were meant to be. The answers will come in time." Apollo's voice, smooth and calm.

Sofia turned to face him, dismayed to find his presence no longer next to her. She craned her neck to find him in the sea of faces, only to discover he was on the gangplank, boarding his ship with Ishmael on his heels. His men, filing after him, no words spoken amongst any of the men. They did their job and back to their ship they went. Sofia saw a dark figure moving beside her and spun around, sword pointing at Marco, Black Heart's second in command and the new captain of the ship.

"I mean you no harm. I hope you intend the same." He smirked, glancing at the body of this former captain.

Sofia nodded and lowered her bloody sword. "Apollo asked my crew and I to escort you and your men here back to Barbados to your ship and crew. I gave him my word!"

He didn't wait for Sofia to respond, before commanding his men to remove the captain and make the body ready for proper burial.

"Do you intend to avenge your captain's death?" Sofia asked, leery of any man serving under Black Heart.

"No, I do not!" Marco took an audible breath, "He had an obsession with you I never understood, he hated and revered you, it made him careless and he dragged the rest of us into his sickness!"

Sofia exhaled in relief. "You mentioned I saved your life, when was that?" She asked softly, turning to look at the new captain of the *Black Revenge.*

Marco nodded, "It was about three years ago when the Captain led a charge against you and your men for your rum, on the island of Nassau. I never forgot you stopped your men from killing me and allowed me to go free." He nodded, then held his hand out, in an act of civility. The corners of Sofia's mouth inched upwards, she nodded back and accepted his hand, marking the end of a long-running feud between ships.

"I would like to take the kid with me." She said, presumptuously.

"The kid?" Marco squinted his eyes in thought, "You mean Red, the slave?"

"I do, but I don't want him as a slave, I want him as a member of my crew." She pronounced.

Marco looked at Sofia, amused by the request. "You may take the boy."

Before she had the chance to respond, Red emerged, grabbing Marco and embracing him in an excited hug. She smiled, briefly shaking her head at Red's excitement and Marco's reaction to the hug. She grabbed Red by the collar, pulling him next to her. The young Scot stayed close to Sofia the rest of the way to Barbados. He slept at the door of the cabin she was in and she was never out of his sight during the day. She spent much of the trip in silence, other than the occasional conversation with the *Black Revenge*'s new captain. She was becoming increasingly frustrated, replaying Apollo's words, not able to finish the conversation, let alone get the orb or answers from the illusive black ghost.

Upon arriving in Barbados, Sofia led her men off the *Black Revenge*, calling to Captain Marco Polo Mancini, "I thank you and release you from your debt."

The new captain smiled and bowed, "Thank you, my lady…" he raised his head slightly, catching Sofia's gaze, "Captain! You are a worthy adversary and truly honorable." He rose slowly, holding her gaze, waiting for her response or at least a reaction.

"This is truly an encounter I won't soon forget!" She exclaimed. "And I'm grateful to you!" With those words she stepped off the gangplank, leaving years of torturous games, death and harassment in her wake.

❈ ❈ ❈

Months went by, Sofia ordered the plundering of ship after ship. *The Margola* spent only time enough on land for repairs, restocking and just long enough for Sofia to meet with Tobias for their load to transport or for payment. She had not granted her crew a full 24 hours on land since just after Black Heart took her prisoner. *The Margola* was in for major repairs on Barbados. There was something changed in her. She was angry, frustrated, the regularity of adrenaline rushes masked her despair over Apollo and the orb. Apollo was truly the Black Ghost. Even Benny and Hugh, who Apollo ordered to remain with Sofia, had no clue of his whereabouts.

"You don't find Apollo, he finds you." Benny would say every time the guessing game of where in the world is Apollo was played. Mac, the closest to Sofia, kept his distance, realizing this was something she needed to sort out on her own. It wasn't until the rumblings of the crew's despondent feelings became too overwhelming to ignore that Mac felt it was time. She was, as she had been for weeks, standing alone on deck near the rail, watching the sun disappear into the horizon.

"Took you long enough." She didn't turn to face him, as she uttered the words, but he could tell she was smiling. "I'm shocked you let me go this long without saying something."

"You were waiting for me, were you?" He asked playfully, the first time in months he felt close enough to her for more than nodding at her orders.

"Maybe I didn't need this much time to calm myself." She gave a little sigh, then turned to him, "You're always the voice of reason when it comes to me. Why didn't you try talking to me sooner?" She quickly looked back towards the horizon, as the sun folded into the crease.

He laughed slightly to himself, thinking about the past couple of months and how intense she'd been, nobody dared to go near her, not even him.

"Well…" he took a breath, "after you managed to not only stay alive but kill one of the most notorious pirates, the crew is a bit wearier of you. Besides, you've been ill-tempered and armed at all times.

She shot him a menacing glance, then started laughing. "I rather like the fact they fear me; although it comes with a sense of longing and loneliness. If I hadn't killed Black Heart, he would have killed me and went after *The Magola*." She gazed down at the rail beneath her hands, lost in introspective thought. "It's the end of some stability." Her body jolted upwards, shocked at her own revelation; bad enough to have such a thought but to hear the words "end of stability" when referring to the death of Captain Tyberias "Black Heart" Keen was completely unexpected.

She glanced in Mac's direction, seeing him dawning his confused sideways look. "Stability? That's what you call the man who couldn't wait to see you dead; following us around the Earth, tormenting you? Stability!" There was an edge to his voice, but after a long pause, including a series of contorted expressions with his mouth, he laughed at the absurdity of it all.

"There was simplicity to it." She argued, over her initial shock. "I knew what to expect. I knew what kind of a man he was and what he was capable of doing. There's not a thing simple about Apollo, the orbs, my connection to any of it." She shifted her eyes back to the horizon. For the first time Mac understood. She had spent her entire pirate life engaged in a cat-and-mouse game with Tyberias "Black Heart" Keen and when it ended, she was sent adrift; forced to deal with an overwhelming cascade of information about her bloodline and faced with an uncertain future.

"I haven't been all that friendly with the crew since that day, have I?" She questioned suddenly, turning back towards Mac.

"No." He answered, simply. "I don't think they're ready to leave you. But you might want to make amends with the crew." He added, mouth turned upwards, relieved to have her back to pre-Black Heart killing.

Chapter 18

They arrived in Barbados, under clear blue skies, sun working its' way down to the horizon. Just as Sofia was about to step onto the gangplank, she was startled by Tobias' presence.

"It's good to see you Captain Rose," Tobias gave a quick bow and motioned Sofia to follow him.

"I thought we were to meet in our usual place?" She glanced at him skeptically.

He uncharacteristically moved closer to her and leaned in, though several inches shorter than she, he bowed his head. "They took him." He whispered, barely audible but with his characteristic emotionless way of speaking.

"Who, Tobias? Took who and who are they?" Sofia questioned, trying to match his volume level, as to not attract the crew's attention.

"My son, Toby, he's 10 years old. Do you recall Jack Horngold?"

Sofia nodded at the recollection of the pirate who confronted Tobias in the pub, demanding their load of rum, her first introduction to Hugh and Benny and the bloodshed that took place.

"It was you!" She said softly, catching the intensity of his hazel gaze, referring to Horngold's mysterious murder the very next day. Tobias held his gaze, neither confirming nor denying but she knew and she instantly understood why the boy was taken.

"Horngold's sons." Tobias paused, voice as calm and emotionless as usual.

"They took him then." Sofia finished, recognizing the strain Tobias was under. Tobias stood motionless, finally nodding slowly.

"Do you know where they've taken him?" She asked, eyeing Mac huddled in a seemingly deep conversation with Hugh, Benny and Jessiah.

"I have an idea of where they might be," he said slowly. Just then, the men broke their huddle and started across the deck towards Sofia and Tobias.

"I knew it wouldn't be long!" She told Tobias, and he nodded, surrendering to the discomfort he felt in having his personal affairs aired to strangers.

"Porcus" Tobias uttered, clearly and slowly.

"Aye, of course it's Porcus!" Sofia laughed, turning her head to the clouds, "You haven't put me through enough?" she pointed a finger up to the sky, shaking her head at the irony of this all.

"Why in the devil are we going to that forsaken island?" Mac inquired, under protest. Porcus was named so for the hundreds of wild pigs roaming freely, both on the island itself and joyfully swimming in the surrounding waters. There was talk of some pirate factions using Porcus, as a place to hide their bounty and some, even as their lair, off the grid. The pigs presented such a problem, most pirates simply took their losses.

"A couple of years back, we went to Porcus in search of gold, rumored to have been buried on the top of the highest mountain peak. Remember that, Sofia?" Mac asked, with a slight laugh at the memory.

"How can I forget," she responded dryly, shaking her head and rolling her eyes.

"We didn't get past the beach with all those beasts chasing us." Mac continued, laughing in-between telling of the account. "Half the crew refused to even get off the blasted ship, I still don't know how we made it off without losing limbs and life to those wild, filthy beasts." He laughed again.

Sofia and Tobias turned towards each other; Tobias nodded in approval. "Jack Horngold's kids took Tobias' son!" Sofia answered, solemnly.

"What? Tobias, young Toby?" Hugh bellowed, expressing an unusual emotional reaction.

"Aye," Sofia focused on Hugh, cocked her head slightly bewildered at the typically mellow Scotsman. Hugh stepped in front of Tobias, quickly followed by Benny, pulled his sword out, knelt down in front of the Jewish/Dutchman and pledged he would get young Toby back alive. Tobias gently touched Hugh's shoulder, uttering several words in Gaelic and ended with Hugh rising and swiftly departing *The Margola* with Benny close on heel. Mac and Sofia turned to Tobias, dawning perplexed looks.

"They went into town for some…supplies," he maintained his usual composure but was clearly withholding information. Recognizing Sofia's uneasiness with the less-than subtle secrecy, Tobias offered up some explanation on Hugh's reaction.

"He's Toby's godfather! Hugh loves the boy as his own." Tobias explained.

"I've not seen him react with such concern over another being before!" Sofia stated. Tobias nodded, but didn't engage further, looking out to the horizon.

❊❊❊

The crew was allowed to go into town but expected back on board just after dawn, allowing for minor repairs, unloading and restocking of the ship, and the return of Hugh and Benny from whatever errand Tobias had sent them on. Sofia knew all too well Hugh and Benny didn't serve at her pleasure, they served at Apollo's pleasure and evidently their bond with Tobias was just as strong.

Hugh and Benny returned on board *The Margola*, sometime in the dark of night. The rest of the crew were back on board and readying the ship to sail by dawn.

"Porcus, here we come!" Sofia shouted, from the center of the deck, a hint of amusement in her booming voice. It was a day over a week before the crow's nest spotted the island and not long afterwards came the first sightings of the wild pigs. Much of the crew had gathered around the sides of the ship, trying to catch a glimpse of the wild animals swimming around. As they inched closer, their squeals hitched onto the backs of the wind.

Tobias was standing alone, leering at the island with such intensity, and Sofia hesitating in interrupting him. "It's all my fault." he uttered, sensing her presence.

Sofia stood, not knowing what to say. "It's not your fault, it is the world we live!" She tried to sound more empathetic but it simply didn't come as natural as sword fighting. Just as she went to step forward, Mac reached out and grabbed her by the arm.

"What are you doing?" She whispered, clearly agitated!

"While you are greatly talented at many things, caring for another person's feelings isn't one of those talents." He crossed his arms righteously.

"Fine, you go to him and see if you can cheer him up!" She ordered, punching Mac hard across the shoulder, as she walked past. He grunted, glaring at her as she walked past.

The squealing was reverberating throughout the air, guiding *The Margola* to the island where hundreds more of the barrel-snouted, large-eared, big-bodied creatures anxiously waited. There was an eerie silence on board, as the men examined the wild beasts from the safety of the deck.

"I think there are more of them than the last time we were here." Jessiah pointed out.

"Aye, I think so too!" Sofia added, suppressing a nervous laugh.

The crew started gathering weapons and the oat slop they had the cook make for distracting the ravenous beasts.

"This is the same slop the cook feeds us!" Jessiah pointed out, as he tipped over the pot, waiting for it to plop into the bottom of a cut barrel.

Sofia shot him a disapproving gaze. "Not the time, Jed!" She called out, while grabbing neatly packed bags of gun powder.

Hugh and Benny, notably absent from the antics and missed opportunities for pranks, were huddled in the corner with Tobias. Sofia glanced over their way, eyes narrowed in frustration over the secrecy and sensing they were purposefully omitting vital information.

Several crew members made their way down the gangplank, while two pirates stood as sentries, at the ready, in keeping the beasts from running up the gangplank. They were quickly met with squeals and grunts and sand flying hastily around, forming a cloud of dust.

"Here we go!" Sofia uttered, barely audible, staring at the mountain, spying the crevice of the cave, supposedly housing young Toby.

"Are ya ready?" Mac asked, joining Sofia.

"Something isn't right." she leaned closer to Mac, keeping her voice down, "He isn't telling us everything and did you see the way Hugh and Benny have been behaving?" She turned, facing him, head slightly cocked, still trying to figure out what she was missing.

"Do you really think there's a problem?" Mac had grown to trust her intuition and often forced her to act on it, as she was naturally impulsive. She simply nodded her answer, slowly and thoughtfully. "It's too late! It's started but be careful!" He said hastily, as the first wave of crew ran down the gangplank, with diversions of food and hand-made traps. Sofia nodded, gave a nervous smile and ran down the gangplank, sword and dagger at the ready. Mac took a deep breath and followed closely behind. There was a cacophony of grunts, squeals, and hooves whipping up sand and men screaming, as they made their way down to the shore. Sofia, Mac, Jessiah, Hugh, Benny and Tobias zig-zagged their way through the flurry of men and beasts, starting their way up the rough tropical mountain.

"Be on the lookout for pigs!" Sofia uttered, leading the group, expecting movement through the brush. Mac stayed close to Sofia, while Hugh, Benny and Tobias, at times, fell behind. Sofia kept glancing up towards the cave, unable to shake off the feeling something wasn't right about all this. Tobias was generally a very honest man but she had come to see a different side, a much darker side. Lost in the preoccupation of Tobias and what awaited them in the cave, she never heard the pack of wild hogs until they were charging right at them.

Benny, usually the furthest back of the four, was first to spin around, confronting the wild beasts with his dagger. The group of large, rowdy swine rocked the short Irishman off balance, as they charged past. He looked like a marionette, someone pulling his strings, as he robotically stabbed the air in-between the hogs, while hopping from one foot to the other.

"Sofia!" Mac cried out, inches from reaching her, as he was knocked over by a notably smaller, less-crazed hog. Shaken, but not hurt, Mac stayed low to the ground, using both hands and feet to flee the stampeders route. Sofia spun around, and immediately registering the danger, used her long muscular legs to catapult herself out of the hogs' path, hitting the ground in a graceful roll.

"You all right, Captain?" Hugh stood over her, hand extended, ready to assist her to her feet.

"Aye," she barely got the word out, as she sat with her hands planted on the ground, holding herself upright, while her body shook with laughter. Hugh looked at her, then quickly surveyed their surroundings and back to Sofia. Seeing the absurdity of their situation, he too doubled-over with laughter.

A much-needed spontaneous release for the both of them. Sofia's laughter tapered off, she lifted to her knees and sprang up. The wild hogs had passed, leaving Sofia and Hugh on one side of the path and Mac, Tobias and Benny on the other side. Mac, relieved to see Sofia unharmed, took a deep breath, reconnecting with them on the path as they continued to climb.

Chapter 19

Sofia held up her hand, signaling them to stop and they followed her lead in crouching down behind the hearty, leafy trees.

"That's John Horngold and the other one there is his brother, Michael. I don't know the others." Hugh whispered, moving closer to Sofia. There were dozens of men around the outside of the cave's opening. The brothers and four of their men were strategically huddled together, backs turned, facing the cave, while the others were spread out. "Perhaps the last brother is in the cave with young Toby." he added.

Tobias was inching towards Sofia, expressionless, not uttering one word since they left the ship.

"Tobias, now is a good time to tell me what we are about to get into. I know there's more to this than you're telling me, so what is it?" She pressed.

There was no response, not even a glance her way. Her senses heightened, she knew he had them walking into a trap. She knew, and impulsively decided it was time to spring it. She jumped up, sword and dagger securely placed on her hips, and walked straight up to the men. They had their backs turned, so she didn't notice the swords in hand and guns at the ready. They spun around, a gun aimed at her head and two swords aimed at her chest.

"We've been waiting for this day! The capture of Captain Sofia Bonny Rose!" John Horngold, the eldest of the three brothers, walked over to her, cautiously taking her sword and dagger and tying her hands together.

Mac went to jump up after her but Hugh and Benny pulled him back down.

Tobias calmly stood and walked towards the men. "I did as you men requested. Where's my boy?" His voice stern, steady but still lacking any emotion. Sofia, unvexed by her current situation, eyed Tobias, as he steadily moved forward towards the front of the cave.

"In there!" John Horngold, pointed to the cave.

"Bring him out." Tobias ordered, voice not rising a single octave.

The Horngold brothers shared a brief glance, Sofia caught on.

"He isn't here." She said, slightly turning her head in Tobias' direction.

The brothers stood there staring at each other, not having thought through their scheme past capture. It took only seconds for Tobias to recognize she was right. He set in motion his backup plan with a simple whistle. Before he finished whistling, scores of pirates hiding in the tropical greens rushed out, wielding swords and guns.

Sofia recognized the big black man standing in the brush, it was Apollo and now she registered what Tobias and the boys had been withholding. He had Hugh and Benny find Apollo; for months they assured her they didn't know where he was, he couldn't be found, if he didn't want finding. They clearly had ways of reaching him, of knowing where he'd be. Things started making sense to her now, as she was the target, she was the reason young Toby was taken. She was a constant target, being a woman and a prolific plunderer. The Horngold brothers used their father's murder by Tobias, as motive behind Sofia.

Watching, as Apollo's men mowed down the Horngold brother's men, she sat simmering in a pot of betrayal, mistrust, and lies by omission, which was coming to a rapid boil. They had bound her hands together in front of her, as her temper rose to uncontrollable heights, the thin rope showed signs of fraying. The brothers grabbed Sofia by the arms, dragging her as she continued to work at loosening the rope binding her hands. She pretended to faint, dragging Michael Horngold down to the ground, she repeatedly kicked him in the face, crawling over to his fallen sword.

"Don't try anything else if ya don't want your head blown off!" The elder brother hissed through his teeth. She halted, feeling the nozzle of the gun against the back of her head. Her long, flowing hair, mangled in the struggle, covered in dirt and minuscule rocks. He grabbed her by the back of her hair, hand fumbling for her neck, dragging her up to her knees. She stood by herself from there. Michael Horngold, brushing himself off, marched up to her, and slapping her across the face, her head jerked from the force, blood streaming down from her nose.

"Let's go!" The elder brother pushed her, with the gun to her back, down the mountain, and Michael walking alongside her, sword pointed at her waist.

"Where's Sofia?" Mac asked Benny, after Horngold's men had been killed.

"They won't get far with her!" Benny stated, without concern, focusing on the cave. Before Mac could get another word out, Hugh and Tobias came out of the cave, Tobias carrying a small-sized shirt.

Mac marched up to Tobias. "This is all your doing! You asked her for help and led her into a trap!" Mac was so enraged, he found spit flying out of his mouth.

Tobias didn't respond, never looked up from the shirt he was gingerly holding. Hugh stood in front of Tobias, drawing Mac's ire away. "Apollo is close, he won't let any harm come to her. Tobias had no choice, the Horngold brothers said they would kill young Toby, if he didn't give them Sofia. He had us give word to Apollo!" Hugh added.

"And what did ya get for betraying Sofia and putting the crew in danger? I don't care about me but I do for the rest of the crew and certainly for her!" Mac responded fervently. "The child's not even here, so all this for nothing!"

"Nothing? Nothing? What if it were your child? Would ya not go to the far ends of the Earth to save him? And, no, we did'na betray her, we had a backup to protect her and the crew!" Hugh fired back, clutching his fists, angry and frustrated.

"We had a backup? We? I see, you and Benny faked loyalty to her, to *The Margola*..."

Hugh's eyes bulged with rage, as his fist made contact with Mac's cheek. "We are loyal to Sofia, but we serve at the pleasure of Apollo and she vera' well knows it! Do ya no recall she was looking for us when Apollo asked us to go with her?" He said, standing over Mac, who was bending over, catching his breath. "We met her in service to Tobias, and she vera' well knows our feelings about him. Did ye no think of that!" He added, slowly lowering his voice.

"Aye!" Mac nodded, catching his breath; gingerly touching his cheek. Hugh held out a hand.

Mac let out a sigh but ignored Hugh's hand and started down the mountain in the direction Sofia was taken. He was more focused than ever, making his way after the Horngold brothers.

Sofia sensed someone in the brush, tracking them, hunting them, but she made no attempt to glance in their direction, so as to not alert her captives. Sofia and John Horngold hadn't noticed Michael no longer beside them. John, preoccupied with keeping the gun in Sofia's back, had not noticed his brother's disappearance for several minutes. Sofia realized about a half minute prior but made no attempt to alert John Horngold, as she sensed it was the work of the Black Ghost himself.

"Michael! Michael!" Panic began setting in, as he realized Michael was gone and not of his own will. Someone was out there, so instinctively he placed the gun in his belt, grabbed his dagger and seized Sofia around the neck. "Show yourself! Do it or she dies!" He screamed, with such an ear-splitting pitch.

Apollo stepped in front of them, point of the sword casually resting on the dirt, his nightly hand loosely holding hilt. "Let her go and I might let you leave this god-forsaken island or ya can choose pig food! I promised these buggers I'd leave them some treats." Apollo said, toying with him, knowing he could kill this man before him without breaking a sweat.

There was something terrifying about Apollo, Sofia thought to herself. She sensed John Horngold's panic, she felt the rapid drum-like bangs of his heart, knowing he was trapped, trapped by his own doing. Droplets of sweat flowed freely from him, soaking Sofia's face, neck and clothes. She felt him start to shift, slightly lowering the knife. Without hesitation, she grabbed his arm wielding the dagger. His arm went limp, and she spun around to him collapsing, lifeless. She grabbed him, stopping the gravitational pull controlling his lifeless body and eased him to the ground, noticing a small hole in the middle of his eyes. She turned, eyeing Apollo, still with a cylindrical object protruding from his dark lips. It was some type of small rock or pellet, propelled by his warm breath she thought to herself. He pulled the cylindrical object from his mouth and placed it back into a pouch, hidden inside his shirt.

"Why are you here?" She asked, marching up to him, gazing upwards into his deep brown eyes.

"Making sure no harm comes to you!" His smooth baritone voice, echoing in her ears.

"I don't need your help! What I need are answers and the orb!" Sofia's voice, higher pitched than usual, found herself uncharacteristically and uncontrollably shouting, drowning in a rising tide of frustration and anger and wrestling wide ranges of emotions from the events of the day.

"Ishmael!" He called out, seeing best to allow calmer tempers before responding. Ishmael walked into the clearing, eating some type of fruit he found in the brush and dragging the spiritless body of Michael Horngold. He laid the body next to the elder brother. Tobias was kneeling at the body, checking for any clues to the whereabouts of young Toby. Sofia turned her head, seeing Mac walking towards them, followed closely by Hugh and Benny.

She turned back towards Apollo taking a deep breath, "I want the orb!" She demanded.

"It's not your time! You aren't ready!" He said, sternly.

"Who are you to say I'm not ready! You don't know me." She uttered, sounding more like a petulant child than the warrior she was.

Apollo leaned forward, "There is a time for everything and a rhythm to life. When you can detect that rhythm, it will be your time." Apollo motioned to Ishmael, who was smartly keeping distance, and the two of them turned to continue down the hill to the pig-covered beach.

"Sofia, when the time comes, I will tell you all!" Apollo called out, stopping briefly, before he and Ishmael disappeared into the greens.

Chapter 20

Back onboard *The Margola*, with Porcus and its' inhabitants safely in their wake, Sofia stood gawking at the island, even after it had vanished from view. She wondered what Apollo meant by "when the time is right". She also wondered why she behaved so differently in his presence, more like an adolescent than a full-grown woman. She was so lost in her thoughts, she hadn't noticed Hugh walking up and standing next to her.

"We never meant ya any harm, lass! Never!" He said, in his Scottish brogue.

She pursed her top lip over her bottom lip, drawing in breath, as means to control her emotions, "I don't blame any of you." She uttered softly. "I don't blame Tobias and I'll still help in getting young Toby back but all you had to do was tell me the truth. I still would have played along but at least I would have been ready!" She confided.

"Aye, we just couldn't take the chance, young Toby is my godson and will probably be the only child I will ever have a chance at having a hand in raising." he finished.

Sofia took a deep breath, "I never said I wasn't going to help get the boy back." she whispered.

Hugh nodded, grinning, taking her words as forgiveness for the betrayal. "Captain, ya need to hear this, you too!" Jessiah called from the door leading inside. "Longfellow overheard one of Hornsgold's men," Jessiah informed them, before entering her cabin.

"Really, Jed, you guys always have to meet in my room?" She asked, with a hint of agitation in her voice. Jessiah grinned sheepishly and moved aside, revealing Mac, Tobias and Benny standing around, and Henry William Longfellow, sitting in a chair.

"Is there an interrogation I'm unaware of, boys?" She laughed slightly at the scene before her.

"Henry here, overhead one of Horngold's men talking about Young Toby." Mac stated cautiously, unsure as to Sofia's reaction. She didn't look in Tobias' direction, stepping in front of him to address Henry directly.

"You can stand, Mr. Longfellow, I'm sure this set-up wasn't intended to make you feel like a suspect." She looked up, giving the men surrounding her a look of displeasure.

"Yes, Captain Rose, I thank you!" He responded, jumping out of his chair.

"What did you hear?" She questioned.

"I hid out of sight, as Jessiah directed me and heard a couple of men talking about a boy with Martin on a small island next to Nassau, No Name Island."

There was a collective audible moan. No Name Island was rumored as the haven for the most vial pirates, the ones on the top of the wanted list by authorities.

"Of course, that's where they're holding him." Sofia shook her head in the irony of this latest news. "If the Horngold brothers didn't have Young Toby on the island, then who is holding him?" She started pacing, as she did when in deep thought. "Who were the Horngold brothers working under?" Adding an additional layer to the mystery.

"Black Fury of the *Revelation*, that's who the men spoke of!" Henry blurted out, remembering the rest of what he had heard.

Sofia spun around in disbelief, while the rest of the room instantly shot skeptical glances at Mr. Longfellow. "He's dead!" Sofia called out defiantly.

"They never recovered his body. There've been rumors he had emerged." Tobias added, speaking for the first time in weeks. The room fell silent, taking in the possibility of Black Fury living and using a child to lure Sofia to him. More chilling for Sofia was the knowledge that Black Fury was the older brother of the former living Tyberias "Black Heart" Keen.

Black Fury's real name was never known just his reputation; he escaped the hangman's noose twice before his younger brother was old enough to sail the seas. It was rumored he was killed in a raid on Nassau years before, but his body never paraded about like the others.

"Thank you, Mr. Longfellow." Creases of her mouth turning upwards, warm and genuine, "I shall never forget how blessed we are to have you, so attentive and helpful!" She added, enjoying the opportune times in displaying her artful conversing abilities. With that, Mr. Longfellow tipped his hat, bowing and excusing himself from the room billowing with impending dread.

"It's about a week, if the weather holds, to No Name." Sofia said, turning to Mac.

"Aye, the wind is working for us right now. Although, we don't have a plan." Mac confided.

"Aye, but we don't know what to expect once we arrive. They will have the tactical advantage, higher ground, time to prepare..." She stopped in mid-thought, thinking about various options for a viable plan. Red, the craftiest at getting in and out of places undetected would swim ashore, scouting the island and all its' inhabitants, then report back to *The Margola*, without capture. It wasn't a complete plan, but a start, she thought to herself. Sofia smiled at the memory of the conversation with Red and the emphasis on him not getting captured or killed. The boy's incredulous reaction to the thought of capture, or worse, provided much-needed levity to the tense room. They had all the weapons at the ready and did daily training with the crew.

The Margola reached Bahamian waters in the black of night, Red was lowered down by rope to the dark, warm waters, rhythmically sloshing back and forth. "Watch him, as long as he's in your sight!" Sofia ordered Jessiah.

"Yes, Captain!"

She went over to the wheel, turning the ship slowly, heading for a little cove, hidden from sight, next to the island. Red had successfully swam to shore undetected. Once on the beach, he moved with remarkable agility, speed and the confidence possessed by a youth. Taking momentary refuge in a small cave, he popped his red head out, listening for sounds traveling on the breeze. He stood for a minute, as a complex web of sounds reverberated around the island. It's voices, he thought to himself, as he was too far away to make out anything beyond that. He surveyed his surroundings, focusing on a path leading deep into the belly of the island. Even if there weren't caves, there seemed sufficient vegetation for him to enshroud himself.

"Waiting is always the worst of it," Sofia uttered, pacing up and down *The Margola*'s deck.

The sun was well above them when Red was spotted and pulled back on board. "Did you see the boy?" Sofia asked, before Red was fully on board.

"No, Captain but he's here. I overheard men talking about bringing food to the boy." He said, gasping for air.

"Well, boy, get on with it, what did ye see!" Hugh demanded, pounding his fist on the side of the ship.

"Aye, sir!" He began, settling onto the ship, sitting on a pile of sacks. "I came upon this cave and…"

"What did ye see, boy! We aren't interested in how you came to what ye saw." Hugh balled up his fists in exasperation.

Red swallowed nervously, taking in a healthy amount of air, "There is a large clearing about a mile in, with several buildings, as far as I can tell, the boy is being held there. There are men for a night watch, about 20 that I saw. But once light came, there had to be 60 men or more milling about." He turned, facing Hugh, waiting for confirmation of a job well done.

Hugh nodded, touching Red's shoulder in silent praise. Sofia stood, arms crossed, contemplating a plan based off of the young Scot's intel.

"Does it seem they are expecting us?" She asked, just as Red was standing up.

"It looks as though they are ready for anything Captain, there are weapons everywhere!"

Sofia exhaled, started to pace. "Can you draw the island, just giving us the lay of the land from where you came upon the shore to the path you took to the clearing and its' surrounding?" She turned, a glimmer in her eyes.

"Aye, I can!" Red said confidently.

Sofia brought in Mr. Longfellow to help Red with the sketches, as she had a hunch, he possessed a fair amount of talent when it came to the arts. The two unlikely partners worked throughout the afternoon, creating a surprisingly real map of the island within their view and beyond.

"We took young Red's recollections and built the island from there." Mr. Longfellow said, standing proudly over the intricate map.

"You both did a fine job! Thank you, now we can use this to make a plan." Sofia smiled at the duo, leading Mr. Longfellow to her door. "Come inside!" She ordered to the group of men standing outside her door in the narrow hallway. Mac, Hugh, Benny, Tobias and Jessiah joined Red in huddling around the newly created map laying on the table in the center of the room.

"This isn't half bad!" Mac exclaimed, tracing the landforms and trails with his finger. The young Scot, hands gently cradling his head, was slumped over the end of the map, exhausted. Sofia caught Hugh and Benny's gaze, revealing that they should head straight for the clearing, housing the buildings.

"These arrows show how Red was able to go undetected, and this is the cave he went into. His estimation is it's large enough to hold 20 men. He said it's not easy to find." She glanced over at Red, still soundly asleep.

"It may not be easy for us to find but Black Fury and his men live there." Mac added. "Yes, but they won't be looking for us, aye?" Sofia countered, eyes sparkling with excitement.

"We hope not!" Jessiah stared at the map skeptically.

"Do ye think his men know we are out here?" Benny inquired.

"No," Jessiah answered quickly, "It's just his reputation precedes him and he's known as one of the smartest among us." He said, slowly and solemnly.

"Even the most sharp-witted amongst us misses things." Sofia glanced over at Tobias, still silent, still lacking emotion, save for clenched fists hanging from his sides.

"Black Fury has been in hiding for years, it may well be he's a bit rusty."

She could tell by Mac's expression that he was pondering her words. His slight nod was all she needed for an agreement. "We take 20 men by dark of night, through the pass, and make our way to this cave, here. From there, the men stay and we, in this room, move ahead to the clearing, before daylight strikes. Red thinks young Toby is likely in this one!" She said, pointing to a small building huddled in the middle of the row of buildings.

"Why that one?" Hugh asked, eyebrows raised.

"A man brought a tray of food in and brought out a pan filled with pee to dump." Red answered, sleepily.

Tobias unclenched his first and lovingly touched the etching of the building.

"Jed, you'll lead the men once we leave the cave. If trouble comes, they are yours to command." She instructed. Jessiah nodded, flashing a quick smile at her confidence in him. Sofia eyed the other men at the table, looking for possible tells of objection to the plan. "Red, you have a couple of hours to get some rest, then you'll be guiding us through to the building."

"Aye, Captain, thank ye," he uttered, head slipping through his hands and smacking onto the edge of the map.

"Oh, leave him, I'm going out onto the deck anyway." Sofia held up her arm, stopping Jessiah and Mac from attempting to disturb Red.

Jessiah chose the men and explained the rescue, as they readied their weapons. Sofia slipped off *The Margola,* followed closely by Mac, Red and the others. Once off, she pushed Red to the front. He had found a small stretch of beach covered by vegetation, reaching out near to where they entered the water from the ship, connecting with No Name Island. They reached the cave with blackness enveloping everything around them.

"Good work, Red!" Sofia whispered, taking a moment to rest on top of a rock just within the lip of the cave.

"Which way now?" Tobias uttered, a little louder than a whisper.

Red popped his head out of the cave, pointing to the right of them. Sofia held her arm out, stopping Tobias from rushing out into the darkness without her and the others. "We're close and I've never known you to be foolish."

He seemed to instantly understand what she was alluding to and stopped short of departing without the group. Red led Sofia, Mac, Tobias, Hugh and Benny out of the cave, down the path he took to the clearing. The deeper they went, the more difficult it was in finding solid footing, with the earth a mix of soft soil, hard rock, thick vegetation and patches of soil and trees. They moved slowly, feeling their way, slowly breathing in the cool, humid, island air. Red made a bird-like noise and everyone froze.

"What it is?" Sofia asked the young Scot.

"The clearing lies about half a mile ahead," she could barely make out the outline of his head and body.

"How do you know?" She asked, skeptically.

"I left this!" He said, untying a swatch of material from a tree next to them.

"Clever boy!" Sofia whispered, through a half smile.

The others had slowly inched up around her and Red, waiting further instructions, "Half a mile to the clearing, is everyone versed on what to do once we are in position?" There was a muffled simultaneous aye, and they continued to the clearing. The black of night was lifting as shadows were emerging in the earliest of morning hours, as the group of rescuers reached the outskirts of the clearing.

Red was squatting down, hands feeling around the earth, "There ye are!" He said, sounding pleased.

"What?" Sofia inquired.

"I placed several rocks in a line, pointing to the building holding the boy," he stood and held his arm up.

"You, stay here, do you understand me?" She turned to Red, now able to clearly see where the boy was physically standing. "Stay out of sight until you see us coming! Do you understand?" She added, narrowing her eyes, straining to see the boy's facial expressions.

"Aye, I understand, Captain." Everyone had caught up and was now surrounding their Captain for further instructions. Sofia was able to make out the outlines of the buildings and she zeroed in on the one Red pointed to.

"It doesn't look like they've had any guards posted around the clearing," she spoke softly, intending for Mac's ears only.

"Aye, it doesn't seem they were expecting company quite yet. I think we are ahead of their schedule." Mac said, leery of what they were walking into.

"Do you think we are walking into another trap?" She asked, not sensing anything of the sort this time.

"I don't know but if the man is anything like the legend; we should expect anything to be possible." He let out a small sigh, "I don't think they are expecting us. I don't think Black Fury ever thought we'd survive the brothers' trap." He whispered. "We need to move. It will be daylight shortly."

Sofia reached over and touched Hugh, Benny and Tobias by the arms. "It's time!" She commanded, with her voice lowered but firm. "The three of you are with Mac and me. Jed, split the men up, half on one side of the clearing and half on the other. If you spot anyone, use the bird call. Once we're out with the boy, high tail it back to the ship!" She looked around, seeing some heads nod in understanding. Without uttering another word, Sofia took off, her tall, slenderly muscular frame crouching down, as much as she could, while maintaining a light gallop across the field. Mac, Hugh, Benny and Tobias followed closely behind, weary of Black Fury's men. Jessiah motioned to the men waiting on the other end of the clearing and both groups moved in perfect unison, flanking their Captain. There was nothing shielding Sofia and her lot, but there were trees and shrubbery on both sides of the clearing, where the rest of her men were. They reached a point of no return with the building plain in site, she had her dagger in one hand and sword in the other, as did her men. A sharp bird sound shocked the silence of the early morning hours. Sofia froze and looked up to find a newly-awakened pirate standing at the door of the building. She went down to her stomach and the rest of the men followed suit, inching along in a crawl through the soft tall grass. She got to her knees, trying to stay as low as she could, motioning to Hugh and Benny for them to break off to the right. Both men nodded, Tobias following close behind them. Sofia waited, as the men moved swiftly, making their way to the backside of the buildings. She watched as a tall figure emerged, recognizing Hugh's shape, taking his place. Something grabbed the pirate's attention, as he slowly turned and headed to the back of the primitive stone dwelling.

Moments later Hugh signaled, all clear and Sofia sprung up from the grass, running to the side of the building, while the others stayed silent and still. A plump, shorter pirate emerged from the closest dwelling to Sofia, his stomping getting louder, as he was coming towards her. She bent down and grabbed the largest rock at her feet. As he was upon her, she jumped out and, with all the strength she could muster, smashed the rock over his head. He collapsed, more graceful than she imagined such a rotund man could be. After witnessing that, Mac sprinted towards her, helping her move the rotund man out of site.

"We need to get the boy and get out of here!" She mouthed, little sound coming out, as they crouched over the body. Mac nodded and made his way to the front of the building, looking back and forth for more awakened pirates. Sofia went around to the other side, meeting him on the other side of the door, both nodding and rushing in the small doorframe. Young Toby lay asleep on a large oval sack, a blanket covering him. Mac ran over, put his hand over the boy's mouth. Whispering in his ear, he could feel the boy's heart pounding wildly and see the whites of his eyes from fright. Mac picked the boy up and flung him over his shoulder, like a sack of barley, while Sofia did another check for Black Fury's men.

"Get going with him! I'll be right behind you." She ordered, in a little more than a whisper. Mac broke into a slight jog coming out of the doorway, but he wasn't much more than 10 jogging steps when he heard the clanging of swords. He hastened his steps, reaching Tobias, who had come out of the grass, seeing Mac carrying his son.

"Take him back to the ship, now, and tell them to be ready to sail!" Mac commanded. Tobias grabbed his son and started back to *The Margola*. By the time Mac got back, more of Fury's men joined the fight, prompting Jessiah and the crew to engage. Sofia had blood trickling down the arm of her shirt, as she pulled her sword out of a man's middle.

"It's not mine, I'm well!" She informed Mac, after seeing the fear on his face. He breathed an audible sigh of relief, as the four of them walked quickly together through the middle of the tall grass. "Wrap it up, Jed!" She called out, running towards the side, where there was the most fighting. Mac followed her, while Benny and Hugh went to the other side to help wrap things up, so they could get off the island and away, before Fury mounted a real attack. Within minutes, the small amount of Fury's men were dead, covered up with the tall grasses of the clearing. An ear-piercing scream came from the buildings and Sofia knew instantly, Black Fury had awakened.

Red was right where they left him and he was up and ready, leading Sofia and the men back to *The Margola*, taking a quarter of the time, thanks to the light of day!

"Get ready to sail! Get ready to sail!" She yelled, running over the gangplank, followed closely by the rest of the men. Jessiah, pulling up the rear, could hear Black Fury through the trees and shrubs.

"This isn't the end of it!" He could hear his men running behind them.

"Let's go!" He yelled, as soon as he hit the gangplank. They pulled up, with Sofia back at the helm, then happily headed into open waters and back to Barbados.

"I don't expect that to be the last we'll see or hear of Black Fury, after all he put on quite the elaborate trap to get to me." She eyed Tobias and his son hugging across the deck, suddenly feeling morose for what the child had endured on her account.

"I want to thank ye for doin' all ye did to get Young Toby back!" Hugh said, standing behind Sofia. "It's not your fault!" He added, sensing the responsibility she felt on her broad shoulders.

"Oh, it's not, is it? Am I not the one who killed his brother?" She asked, sardonically.

"He kidnapped you! He was setting you up for assassination and you think you killed him without reason?" She didn't notice Tobias standing there.

"Come on Young Toby, let's go for a walk," Hugh gently touched Sofia's shoulder and grabbed the young boy by the hand, leaving Tobias and Sofia.

"Do you think you killed him without reason?" Tobias asked again, stepping in front of her.

"No, I do not!" She stated, simply looking down at the small man.

"Then how is it you think this is all on your shoulders?" He pushed, not raising his voice one octave, and no hint of agitation, just the same monotoned Tobias.

Sofia took in a large amount of air. "I am responsible, Tobias, I am responsible for all that happens to those surrounding me! Black Heart was obsessed with me and it was a game for years, until he kidnapped me, and I finished him. That awakened a sleeping giant of the pirate world not to mention putting you and my entire crew in jeopardy!" She released the remaining air.

"Captain Rose, you risked your life and crew to rescue my son on two different islands. None of this is your doing and I'm forever in your debt." The small-framed man bowed elegantly and for the first time she witnessed a slight upwards motion of the creases of his mouth. Shocked by the sight of Tobias Jansen smiling, even a slight one, softened her and the load she was carrying lightened.

Chapter 21

The Margola pulled into Barbados in the early morning hours. The crew barely waited for the gangplank to drop, before scurrying into town for much-needed time away from plundering and fighting ghosts of pirates' past. Sofia walked slowly down the gangplank, thoughts focused on one pirate, the living ghost, a connection to her past and possibly her future. Tobias and Young Toby, flanked by Hugh and Benny keeping pace behind her.

"Hugh, a minute please," she said, halting suddenly, Tobias and Benny bringing up the rear, but not yet on solid land. Hugh looked over at Benny, as Benny nodded, silently acknowledging Tobias and his son were in his protection. Hugh followed Sofia out of earshot.

"I want to meet with Apollo." her eyes narrowed, her hands clenching and releasing in a mix of nervous and frustrated energy. "You owe me, do you not? You said so yourself. I want to meet with Apollo!" She took a step forward, only inches separating them.

He nodded slowly and slightly, "You wait for me to come get you. Do ye hear?"

She took a couple of steps back, surprised by the tone in his voice, the slight disrespect. But then she was fully aware she was potentially putting him at odds with his own captain.

"What was that all about?" Mac asked, as he walked up next to her, while she watched Hugh, Benny, Tobias and the young boy disappear down an alley.

"I told him I want to meet with Apollo and that he owes me a debt." she turned, catching Mac's gaze.

He didn't immediately respond, stood looking past her, as if in deep thought. "When?" He simply asked.

"Sometime tonight, Hugh said he'll come for me." she glanced in the direction the boys disappeared with Tobias and his son.

"I'm coming with you and no is not an option!" He said sternly. She nodded slowly in agreement, knowing when he made a declaration such as this there was no changing his mind and she welcomed the support.

"What if you don't like what you find out?" He asked, voice low, filled with concern.

"It will be the truth, there's not a thing I can do about that." She looked down, exhaling as though she was carrying the weight of 10 men.

There were times, not many, but on occasion Sofia let herself show a more vulnerable side and Mac relished lending whatever comfort she was willing to take from him. "Don't slam me to the ground or pull your sword but I'm going to grab your hand." Mac informed her, as he reached out and gently took her hand in his. She let out an audible laugh at the warning and squeezed his hand back.

※※※

Sofia and Mac spent much of the late afternoon and early evening at the tavern Sofia first met Apollo. Sofia anxiously waited for Hugh and Benny to come for them, while Mac enjoyed the whiskey. It was well into the dark of night before Hugh and Benny showed, Sofia had not taken her eyes off the door leading into the tavern since they sat down. And she jumped up the moment Benny poked his head through the tavern door. She tapped Mac's arm in mid-drink, spilling whiskey half down his shirt.

"Hey!" He protested but she was half out the door by the time he settled himself and rose out of his chair. "Damn, exasperating woman." he murmured under his breath, quickening his pace after seeing the door shut with Sofia on the other side. Benny was waiting for him, as Sofia and Hugh were about 20 feet ahead.

"She couldn't wait, not a second, and I had to leave coin for the drinks." He explained to Benny, as he attempted to brush droplets of whiskey from his shirt.

"Aye, Apollo is none too happy with us. It looks like we will be goin' with ya after all when ya set sail tomorrow."

"If he doesn't want to meet, why did he agree to it?" Mac questioned, suddenly serious. "Hugh told him she was'na gonna stop until he answered her. I told him too, it was a matter of time before she tracked him down herself." he explained.

Sofia and Hugh slowed their steps, allowing Mac and Benny to catch up. They walked down one dark alley to another, Hugh and Benny looking for would-be followers. After another couple of blocks, the boys stopped abruptly.

"Here, quickly!" Hugh ordered, as he pushed a brick in the wall of the building before them and a small stairwell emerged. Sofia quickly started down the dark stairway, followed closely by Mac and Benny. Hugh stepped in, pushing another brick on the wall to close the entrance of the stairwell. Sofia stopped at the bottom, waiting in the softly-lit underground.

"This way!" Hugh walked in front of Sofia, leading the group deeper into the underworld.

Candles along the wall dimly illuminated the narrow path. Sofia stretched her hand above her head and ran her fingertips across the underbelly of the street above. It was damp and cold, with a calm and sense of safety she hadn't felt in a very long time. There was a glow at the end of the path, Sofia quickened her pace, forcing Hugh to quicken his. This was not an ordinary glow of dingy yellow candlelight;

the bright white light seemed to speak to her, and she was transfixed by it, like a moth to a flame.

"What is that?" Sofia asked.

Mac stopped, hand on sword. "What?"

"That light." Sofia added. "It's different."

Mac gazed at the light again but saw nothing out of the ordinary. He glanced back at Sofia but she seemed a world away.

The light was now ablaze, as Sofia darted in front of Hugh, entering the room, eyes wide and slightly out of breath. Apollo, divine in build and temperament, stood next to the source of the illumination, the orb. It was about the size of an orange, the room ablaze from its power.

"This is what we've been after? I pictured it much larger." Mac tilted his head, hoping that would somehow make it look different.

"It's magnificent!" She said, her eyes large with wonder; pupils dancing to the light radiating from the orb, as if someone had plucked a star from the sky and placed it on the table.

The large room had several round tables, lined with chairs and a large bar at the far end, complete with bottles of alcohol.

"Welcome," he said simply, motioning for Sofia to take a seat at the table where the orb sat. "Please make our guests feel welcome." he added, turning to Ishmael, walking into the room from a back doorway. Ishmael led Mac to a larger table, set with four chairs, while Hugh and Benny brought a couple of bottles of rum and glasses to the table. Sofia couldn't take her gaze off the glowing orb, her mouth hung slightly open, as she took a seat at a small round table across from Apollo.

"You are part of a group of people…" he started, catching Sofia's intense gaze fixed on his every word.

"Yes, go on," she insisted, leaning her tall, slenderly, muscular frame over the table in complete focus and attention.

"Your parents were futurists." He said, speaking softly and slowly, his voice deep, smooth and commanding. "The orbs…"

"Orbs? Wait, there are more than this one?" Sofia asked, cutting him off.

"There are four; they came out of the earth years ago and only work when the four are united. The orbs speak to the Futurists in forms of flashes of future events. Only those with the power can see the bright glow and the visions it projects!"

She looked past Apollo to Hugh and Benny sitting at the other table. "You see the light of the orbs, right?" There was an arc to her voice, "It's a beam of white light; surely you can see it." Her voice trailed off at the end, seeing their bewildered faces. She met Mac's eyes and he nodded slightly, with a slight crooked smiled meant to reassure her all was fine. Sofia turned back to the orb; her eyes fixed on the glowing light; wanting Apollo to continue but dreading his words.

"I know this is a lot child," he started, his voice suddenly soft, filled with gently empathetic tones, "If you'll allow me to continue, things will start making sense." She nodded, with some hesitation, caught completely off-guard by his sudden tenderness.

"A woman found the orbs in a cave long ago; they were glowing and flashing images of a massacre, as she approached them. Many were killed the following week in the area the flashes foretold. The presence of the orbs drew others like her to it and together they formed a secret society of Futurists. They took a vow to alter the future for the better and they have!"

"What happened with them?" She stumbled, her mind struggling to process Apollo's words. "Where do my parents connect in all this?" She questioned.

"Your mother was the woman and your father was one of the ones drawn to the orb. They formed the society and led the Futurists." Apollo stopped, looking at Sofia, sitting there stoic, learning of her bloodline and her place in the world.

"What happened to the group," she asked, clearing her throat, speaking uncharacteristically soft.

"There was a traitor amongst The Futurists, a pirate in Fury's command. Black Fury and his men waged war on The Futurists, vowing to steel the four orbs. Your parents separated the orbs, assigned a protector to each of them, making it nearly impossible for Fury and his men to locate all of them. Your parents were taking the orb to the colonies for safety. The *Black Revenge* came upon them before they could ever reach the colonies. The *Captiana Mia* put up such a fight, firing upon the Black Revenge, leaving Black Heart no choice but to fire back, sinking them." Apollo stopped talking, and Sofia held his gaze, his eyes showing an empathy she hadn't seen before.

"Wait, are you saying Black Heart killed my parents."

"Under orders from his brother." He slowly nodded.

She placed her hands on her chin, her long fingers covering her full, pink lips. The pieces of her existence coming together with every word she was hearing. "Are you a Futurist too?" Sofia asked, moving her fingers down to her chin.

"No, I am the sworn protector of the Futurists and its' cause." He stated simply.

Sofia pondered his words for a moment, "You cannot see the light from the orb or the flashes of the images when the four are together?"

Apollo shook his head. She nodded in understanding, a cacophony of emotions ringing in her ears, ranging from excitement to disbelief. She always felt different, born to chart a course few took, and course even fewer women dared to think of. She towered over most girls growing up, fought more fiercely than most boys; born a force to be reckoned with and now, after all these years, learning the beginnings of why.

"What is this place?" She asked, after several introspective moments, now ready to change the subject.

"I wanted a place on land, but you see, I'm a wanted man with many enemies."

"And friends." Sofia added quickly, flashing a soft smile. He returned with a slight smile and nod.

"Mr. Mac, Mr. Hugh, Mr. Benny, please come join us." He uttered, without looking over to the men who were draining the second bottle of rum. The three men walked over to the table and took their seats. "Now then, we have a bit of business to figure out." Apollo started, narrowing his eyes at Hugh and Benny. Both men, catching Apollo's menacing gaze, promptly stood at attention.

"Apollo, I'm the one who insisted on them bringing me to you, please, this is between you and I." She rose, instinctively placing her hand on her sword.

Apollo cocked his head to one side, reflecting on the current state of his men and the Captain standing at their defense. A master player of games and quite cognizant of his reputation, Apollo couldn't resist teaching lessons where lessons were required. He remained silent, seeming pensive as Hugh and Benny stood as stones and Sofia's eyes were narrowed, fingers gently touching the hilt of her sword.

"Let me ask you…," he started breaking minutes of tense silence, "If two of your men disobeyed you by bringing someone to you, what would you do to them?"

Sofia glanced back at the men, then over at Mac.

He smirked, ever so slightly, and raised his glass to his mouth to cover it, enjoying the show, recognizing Apollo's play.

She turned her attention back to Apollo, now sitting up straight in the chair, anticipating her response. She bit her lip, reflexively, "That depends on whether their disobedience was to protect me or have benefit to me." She smiled, wide as a Cheshire Cat.

Apollo burst out laughing, leaning forward, with his hands on his head. Hugh and Benny were chuckling behind her and Mac's face broke out in a grin from ear to ear.

"You're messing with me!" She shouted, suppressing the urge to smile.

"Aye child, I am! They know well when I'm truly serious and when I might be convinced otherwise! I have followed you your entire life, so when it comes to you, all is forgiven." He said, holding his hand up, signaling his men to sit.

She eyed him, conflicting emotions whirling inside of her,
"Black Heart and Black Fury have been after the orbs for years. Now that you killed his brother, Fury will not stop coming after you. It's no longer about getting the orbs; he'll also want his revenge." Apollo said, thinking out loud.

"You want me to play the bait?" Sofia asked incredulously, picking up on Apollo's train of thought. Sofia thought about how many times she'd been captured and couldn't help but chuckle. "Where are the other orbs?" She asked, patiently waiting for Apollo to get out of his own thoughts. "One is in the colonies, another on an island near the convict colony of Australia." he looked up at Sofia and drew in breath, "Black Heart tracked one down on an island near Italy and murdered its' protector, Fury has that orb." He said, barely audible.

"How? How do you know that?" She asked, moving her pointer finger back and forth, reflexively, across her lips.

"I had a man embedded in with Black Heart, and after you killed him, his crew went back under Fury's direct command. He was immediately discovered, a letter found on him from the protector; it gave up the Futurist's location and the Futurist was killed after he was. Fury has the orb. Fury had suspected him for a while but Black Heart took a particular liking to him and with that came protection from his brother.

"Marco, his name was Marco Pollo Mancini, wasn't it?" She looked over at Apollo, knowing the answer but hoping it wasn't so.

"How do you know that?" He asked, eyes narrowed, stiffening his back.

She turned away, staring at the blank wall, "He's the one who helped save my life on the ship, before you boarded. He said he owed me for saving his life, sometime ago." She pursed her lips together, "But that never happened, did it? He helped save my life because he was one of your men."

"Yes!" He agreed. "He's dead because of Fury, not you." he added, sensing her guilt. "I did not know he made contact with you on the ship. He was clever; set things in motion without a soul knowing he was behind them. He was careful to not blow his true loyalties; he rose through the ranks with Keen quickly, giving him valuable access to information but putting his life at more risk. He was a good man." Apollo sat back in remembrance.

She knew he was right. She was grateful to Marco and would never forget what he did for her.

Sofia placed the orb in a small blanket, wrapped it as if it were a small baby, cradling it in her long muscular arms. "That's a good look on you!" Mac said, flashing a smile. She shot him back a menacing look, then quickly turned her attention back to the bundle in her arms, smiling at the thought. Apollo handed her paper with coordinates of the Futurists harboring the orbs, along with a carefully-wrapped package.

"Open it on your ship." He ordered, creases of his mouth slowly turning upwards, softening his rough features. She looked at him, eyes sparkling, smiling back at him, feeling oddly connected. It was well into the middle of the night when Hugh, Benny, Mac and Sofia slipped back onto the dark street, quickly making their way back onboard *The Margola*.

Chapter 22

Sofia sat in her cabin, staring at the package given to her by Apollo, the orb wrapped in material and placed in a circular scarf hanging around her neck, resting comfortably on her chest. She tore into the package and pulled out an old, black dagger. She caressed the hilt, feeling instantly comfortable with it. Sofia jumped up from her chair, fighting a make-believe foe, slashing the dagger back and forth, lunging forward for the kill.

"Whoa there!" Mac laughed, closing the door, walking close to the wall avoiding the center of the room, where Sofia was still slashing air. "Was that in the package Apollo gave you?" He asked, staying closely by the wall.

"Aye!" She, pulled the dagger up to her eyes, closely examining it. "It's certainly old but there's something about it that feels..." she ran her fingers up and down the hilt, "familiar!"

Mac went over to the table and pulled a neatly folded piece of paper out of the torn wrapping. "Here's a note of some kind," he said, as he held it up.

She grabbed it out of his hand, eyes welled with tears, as she handed it back to Mac and clutched the dagger with more intensity.

Mac read the note out loud, "This belonged to your mother. She left it in the event she couldn't return to you." He gingerly placed the note down next to the torn package. "Well, you've had quite the few days." he said, not really knowing what exactly to say.

The corners of Sofia's mouth turned upwards, tears welled up in her amber eyes, as she gently and fondly caressed the hilt of the dagger.

"So where to?" Mac asked, changing the subject.

"Bali, Apollo said one of The Futurists is on Bali and the other is in the colonies." She said, lifting the dagger up to the beam of sunlight streaming across the room from an opening in the wood panels above.

"Sofia, I'm a fairly-educated man." he started. She turned to him, slowly, dagger glowing in the beam of light. Her eyes narrowed, waiting for the rest of the perplexing statement. "Where in the world is Bali?" He asked, turning a soft shade of pink.

"The Indonesian Archipelago," she said, with a smile.

He shot her a contemptuous look, tapping his foot wildly, the noise echoing throughout the room. She broke out in side-splitting laughter, doubled over, clutching tightly to the dagger. Mac, wanting the appearance of outrage, lost himself in her joyous laughter, started chuckling, evolving into total exuberance.

"Not far from India," she said, clutching her side, with her hand not in possession of the knife.

"The orient?" He questioned, recovering quickly from the laughing episode. Sofia nodded, still grinning from ear to ear.

"Why that's on the other side of the world!" Mac said, dread taking hold of him, thinking about the months at sea. "We don't have enough food for a journey like that. What about damage from storms?" He asked, speaking quickly.

"The route we're taking, there'll be several places for us to restock on food and other needs," she assured him, pulling out the map.

"This is going to take us months!" He took his finger, drawing their route.

"About three and a half months with good winds at our back," she added, watching his finger stop at a cluster of islands.

※ ※ ※

Weeks went by, fair weather and good winds followed by weeks of storms. *The Margola* suffered minor injuries to her deck and masts from the weeks of rain and hail battering the deck and winds lashing the masts.

"Land! Land! Land!" Shouted Jessiah from the crow's nest, slightly leaning to counterbalance. Sofia looked up from securing the damaged wheel with rope, watching Jessiah skillfully navigate the teetering nest, held by a pummeled mast.

"I heard," she said, seeing a slenderly-built shadow draw near. "If we stay the course, we should be there in the next few hours." The shadow growing longer, as its' owner grew closer. "Aye, do we know what land we are coming to?" She asked, rising to her full six-foot height.

"Not the foggiest," Jessiah said simply, shrugging his shoulders. She smirked and looked past him to the visible outline of land, a mirage marked with a light haze lying in the middle of the vastness of blue.

"Captain?" Jessiah waited until she made a sound of acknowledgment within her throat. "What are the orders once ashore?" he questioned, excited to step both feet on solid soil!

"You care for the maintenance of the ship and restocking of provisions. Mac and I will take some men into town to find items for trade." She said, without ever turning around.

"What men do you want with you?"

She turned around, facing him. "Hugh and Benny will go with me, you take Red and Mr. Longfellow, and start showing Red how to take care of the ship. Decide who else you want with you."

"Are ya looking to get rid of me?" He asked, with a lack of seriousness.

"Are you looking to leave?" She suppressed the urge to laugh out loud.

"You know I am not!" He said indignantly.

"No, Jed," she smiled, "I'm not looking to replace you, nor ever get rid of you but we need another to take care of the ship." She stopped short of saying anything about the possibility of him getting killed, as she was uncomfortable thinking it and too superstitious to say it out loud.

Chapter 23

Sofia adjusted the orb hanging safely and snugly around her neck, tucking it underneath her shirt. She hadn't taken it off since they left Apollo, sleeping and even bathing with it. She liked going onto land alone but her capture by Black Heart and his men from her own ship had rocked her sense of invincibility. She lightly touched the orb at her chest, feeling a maternal instinct to care for it and see it safe and happily reunited with the others. The connection to her parents was strong within it and she sensed that, embraced it, felt comforted by it. It was nearing dusk when they pulled into port, a sizable port with land extending as far as the eye could see. Sofia stepped off *The Margola*, followed closely by Mac, Hugh and Benny. The streets were filled with merchants, buyers and beggars buying, selling and begging flowers, foods, cloth, clothing and pots. Sofia, mesmerized by the lavish rows of tents, walked casually towards the market, behaving much as the other shoppers but hardly blending in. Standing six-feet tall, cloak covering head to knees, with men flanking her on all sides, she was collecting occasional glances and frequent stares, as she made her way up and down the aisles.

"I don't like this," Mac whispered to Benny, "I have a bad feeling about this place." He confided, trying to keep Sofia from hearing.

"Not to worry, who would know she's here, we aren't even sure where we are!" Benny uttered, not understanding the concept of whispering. Something caught her eye, a table filled with small, round, spherical objects. Slowly, she went up to the table, picked up one and examined it closely.

"It's a mini replica of the orb," she whispered to Mac.

"Coincidence, you think?" He asked, pulse rapidly accelerating, drops of sweat forming on his brows.

She shook her head slowly, eyeing a pair of dark, beady eyes peering from behind a small, cloth structure. She carefully placed the mini orb back onto the table and held the gaze of the eyes, until a short, stout man appeared.

"You know what they are?" The mysterious man asked.

Sofia glanced back at her men and then did a quick survey of the area around them. She leaned in slightly to the small man, nodding slowly. He continued to stare at her for a moment, before advancing closer to the table, removing his magnifying glass over one of his beady little eyes. His eyes lit up, as he stepped into the sun, "It is you. I knew you'd come."

Out of the corners of her eyes, she saw Mac, Hugh and Benny place their hands on their swords in a synchronized motion. "Who is it you think I am?" Sofia said, confidently and softly, feeling glares of eyes on her back.

"You're the daughter!" He pointed at her with a stubby, hairy finger.

Sofia met the man's gaze, *The daughter?* With a round face, protruding ears, a large, short, round nose he reminded her of the nomads going into and out of her town when she was little. She stood perfectly still, waiting for the little man to make his next move. He set his hand on the table and leaned closer to Sofia. Instantly, Mac and Hugh pulled their swords and crossed them over Sofia, and she didn't flinch or move a muscle.

"Back down boys!"

"Ha, it is you!" The man shouted in a whisper, hardly able to contain his excitement.

"Whose daughter do you think I am?" She asked, anxiously.

"Oh, I don't think, I know!" The man laughed. "You're Abigail Grace Faith Rose's daughter." he said leaning over the table, forcing her to bend down.

She stepped back, blood draining from her face, dismayed hearing her mother's full name uttered by anyone, let alone a stranger from some foreign land she'd never been. Mac and Hugh grabbed her arms, holding onto her until color started returning to her face. Benny, anxiously standing with his back to hers, eyes scanning the crowd moving in front of them, removing fears of a surprise attack.

"How do you know my mother's name? How do you know who I am?" She asked, collecting herself.

The odd little man made some peculiar noises, motioning her to bend down again. "I knew your mother!" He whispered, "Your father too!" He added with an eccentric giggle. Suddenly, his face turned serious. "I was a Futurist, until the orbs were split up and we went into hiding. Come with me!" the stubby, plump man waved his hand, beckoning Sofia to follow.

She looked at Mac, shrugging her shoulders and followed, as he, Benny and Hugh followed closely. They went through the canvas opening, walked through the crowds, ending up on a desolate street and into an alley, before slipping into a well-hidden doorway. Sofia had visions of a book she once read; a girl followed a mad rabbit into a hole, leading to a world of twisted imaginations. She giggled at the memory, shattering the silence.

"Funny isn't it, you running into me?" Asked the man, forging ahead in the blackness of the building.

"I don't know if I would call it funny." she remarked, sardonically. There was a light glow at the end of the long hallway, they stepped into a sizable room, where shelves lined the floors, bottom to top filled with books.

"Please and thank you." the man motioned hastily for his guests to sit at a table in the middle of the room. It was set with cups and a large black pot sat in the middle of the table, set neatly for five.

Sofia eyed the table, wearily, "You knew we were coming." she stated, still staring at the place settings. "How did you know?"

He motioned again for them to sit, and Sofia walked over taking a seat, knowing her men would not sit until she did. "I am a Futurist, like I told you. I don't need to rely on the orbs for all my abilities. I'll see flashes here and there but mostly it's intuition, I woke up feeling I was going to have guests from afar. I had no idea it would be you, but I sensed there would be four of you." he said, flashing a smile. "I am O'Rourke." He addressed his audience. "I am a founding member of The Futurists along with your mother and father." he said, bowing his head in Sofia's direction. Every reference to her mother sent a shock wave throughout her body, causing her to visibly twitch in her chair. "You met with Apollo." He stated, not needing a response. "You know pirates were after us, after the orbs themselves and their power. I had one of the orbs and was going to take it back to my homeland, the lovely Irish isles, when I was outed by one of the men on the vessel and we were attacked before we reached open waters. Apollo found out before the attack took place and was able to get to me. He brought me here for my own safety and placed the orb in the care of another Futurist on an island far away." He stopped, reached for the black pot in the middle of the table and poured himself a drink.

"They are still after you?" Sofia asked, her voice seeped in empathy.

"They are that!" He took another sip, thoughts on a past he had no control over and facing a future of seemingly insurmountable odds.

"Why you?" Sofia asked, stiffening her back.

"Black Fury didn't just want the orbs, he wanted to make sure The Futurists were never able to rise up again, so he went after the founders, the leaders." His voice softened, eyes turned, meeting Sofia's gaze. "Rumors were it was Keen, Black Fury's brother, who sank *Captiana Mia*. It has been said your mother fought so gallantly she left Keen no choice than to sink The *Capitana Mia*, the orb lost with them."

Sofia felt her pulse race, her heart was pumping wildly. "Black Heart's dead! He no longer matters." She said, through clenched teeth.

"Black Heart?" O' Rourke snorted, "He was a puppet, strings controlled by his brother. It's him who keeps us hidden. It's him who threatens the orbs and their power!" O'Rourke stood, walked over to one of the shelves, gently touching the bindings of books neatly resting on a shelf measuring his eye level, and stopping on one blue leather-bound book. "Ah, here it is; been a while since I pulled it out." He said triumphantly, wiping the years of dust from its binding. Sofia started pacing up and down the length of the table, fists clenched in frustration, as O'Rourke thumbed through the book at the shelf.

"We'll get Fury!" Mac said, standing at one of her pacing paths.

"Oh, I will!" She said, hastening her steps, making Mac shake his head from the dizzying motions.

Feeling a bit queasy, he grabbed her arm, hard, as she rounded him for the fifth time.

"Let go of me!" She whispered, through clench teeth.

"You're not doing yourself or anyone any good by carrying on!" He whispered, sternly. Hugh and Benny removed themselves from the table, meeting O'Rourke at the shelf.

"You heard him." She jerked her arm free from his grasp. "Fury killed my parents!" She uttered, just audible enough for him to hear.

"We'll get him! We will, just as you got Black Heart, but in due time. First, we have a mission, you said so yourself, we need to unite the orbs." He let go of his grip on her arm, "Apparently you got your fighting skills from your mom!" He flashed a smile, as he turned to find O'Rourke, Hugh and Benny heading back to the table.

"I want to show you this." the little man said, motioning for Sofia to come over, as he laid the book open on the table.

"What is it?" She asked, standing beside O'Rourke.

"This is our history, The Futurists, I mean. Your parents, me, Apollo and a couple of the other founding members wrote this. Your father was quite skilled with the pen, your mother with the sword." Tears welled in his eyes, as he stood skimming through the writings, remembering better days. "I've been alone so long, I've read most these books, cover to cover, but I've not taken this one out since I arrived." He said, wiping the tears away. Sofia gently touched the man's shoulder, feeling the connection stemming from her parents. "In this is why we formed the Futurists and accounts of our servitude, before we disbanded." He lowered his head. "I want you to have it." He said, turning to Sofia.

"I can't take that from you, it belongs in a library, not a pirate ship, where it can be lost or stolen." She said, the corners of her mouth slowly turning upwards.

"It's your history!" He pushed, handing her the book. She picked up the book carefully, with both hands, and started thumbing through it, softly touching the words.

"It's *our* history!" She told him. She thoughtfully and delicately turned page after page, reading parts and skimming others. "Please, keep it here. Keep it safe and when we have the orbs back together and the world is safe from Fury; I'll come for you both." She smiled, handing the book back to O'Rourke.

"You have her soul!" He whispered, as he took the book, walking back to the shelves, placing it in the very spot he took it from.

"We are going to unite the orbs." she repeated, as he was making his way back to the table. She pulled the circular cloth out from her shirt, revealing the orb.

O'Rourke's beady blue eyes grew large at the site of the orb, "Is that the one your parents were taking to the new world?" He asked, outstretching his arm, but halting it mid-air, before touching the orb.

Sofia nodded, "Apollo and his men found the ship, and the orb."

Tears of hope welled in the small, stout man's eyes, as he lowered his arms.

"I'll come back for you, as soon as it's safe for The Futurists!" She bent down and kissed the small man on his head. Too choked up to speak, O'Rourke nodded and watched, as Sofia and her men left the tent, heading back to *The Margola*.

Chapter 24

Sofia had one hand instinctively clutching the orb around her neck, as she tossed and turned, her subconscious working through the depths of distorted images – her only memories of her parents. Flashes of one Captain Tyberias "Black Heart" Keen wove through the images, sending bolts of rage coursing through her veins, her body answering to the pulsating surges.

"Ha, ya foolish girl, it's me ya want. My brother was under my orders! Come and get me!" A voice teased.

She sat up, gasping for air, heart pounding like a drum, muscles twitching like a live electric wire. Her muscles ached, as she slowly and gently stretched her long limbs out. She brushed her long, sweat-soaked hair back with her hands, cautiously laying back down. She closed her eyes, trying to capture whatever visions she could retrieve from her subconscious and ended up drifting to sleep.

❈ ❈ ❈

"Hello Captain Rose!" Mr. Longfellow said, sitting cross-legged on top of several stacks of burlap bags.

"What in the world are you doing up there, Mr. Longfellow?" Sofia asked, a bit startled by the voice from above.

"Sketching and taking in the scenery," he replied contently.

"Carry on then!" She smiled, and shook her head, as she walked past the stacks. Mac was standing with Jessiah, Red and a few of the other men, going over daily duties and inventories, when Sofia walked over.

"Captain!" The men said in unison, tipping their hats. She gave a nod, acknowledging the men, her presence always loomed large and disrupted any sort of current business. She caught Mac's intense gaze and held it, knowing he knew she wasn't sleeping, because he understood the weight she carried and tried to prop her up, as best as he could. The men had resumed chattering. Mac circumvented the gaggle of men, meeting Sofia in a partially-secluded area near the wheel.

"You aren't sleeping!" He said, looking past her, "The nightmares are back?" He asked, turning to her.

"It's always Black Heart, but now, at the end, I hear Fury's voice and he's taunting me, making sure I know it was him who gave the order to go after my parents." She whispered, swallowing hard.

"Black Heart can't hurt you anymore and as far as Fury, well we'll get to him in due time!" He said, gently touching her shoulder.

"I don't fear Keen, I've never feared him! Facing down the barrel of his gun, I still didn't fear him!" She said defiantly, brushing his hand off her shoulder. "I don't fear Fury either!" She added, balling her hands into fists at her sides.

Mac stepped back, eyes narrowing at her, the empathy he had felt noticeably waning. "No, you don't fear either of them, you don't fear anyone! I know that, but you do fear for your men, do you not? Or do you want revenge so badly, you'll act a fool and walk into whatever trap Fury sets? You may not care for yourself but those of us who do care for you have to stand by and watch you be reckless!" His voice was raised, laced with frustration, as he went to walk away.

"Wait!" She said, through clenched teeth, "I am no fool and you know that well! I do want revenge, so badly I can taste it, but I would never put you or the men at risk. As for caring…" she walked up to him and touched his hand, "I know you do." She said simply, the corners of her mouth turned up.

As it was from the moment, he met her, he couldn't stay upset, all was forgiven, as it always was once, she flashed a smile, a moment of unexpected tenderness, and he was back by her side, accepting her just as she was.

❈ ❈ ❈

It had been weeks since they had seen another ship. Jessiah's voice cut through the air, snapping everyone to attention. "Ship! Ship! Ship!"

Sofia was on deck, her long legs landing just under the nest.

"It looks to be a Spanish vessel, Captain!" He shouted.

"Prepare to board!" She ordered, sending the deck into a frenzy! She stared at the ship, as the distance between them quickly shrank, she knew that ship, she'd boarded it before. She boarded hundreds of ships and it was not uncommon for them to rob the same ship multiple times but this one was different, although she just couldn't quite figure out why. Sofia held back, allowing some of her men to secure the ship and begin rummaging through the cargo.

It wasn't until she was standing on the deck, face-to-face with the Captain held at bay by the blade of Jessiah's sword, that she realized why she recognized the ship. "I knew the ship looked familiar!" She said to the captain of the secured ship, with a Cheshire smile.

"I kept my homeland flag down to avoid the likes of you!" Captain Mateo Barroso replied, narrowing his eyes at Sofia, as the blade of Jessiah's sword inched closer to his neck. She held her hand up, signaling Jessiah to lower his sword, as she approached the Spanish captain.

"It's good to see you again, Captain!" She uttered, glancing over to see her men shaking down the crew. "Leave the crew alone! Go down to see what cargo there is but no breaking of things, understand!" She commanded.

"Aye Captain!" The crew replied in thunderous unison, as Mac joined Jessiah and the two of them led half the men to the cargo hold below. The other half remained, watching the *Sao Mateus'* crew with swords drawn.

"What is your purpose here then?" Captain Borosso asked Sofia.

"To take!" She said simply, looking directly at him. Out of the corner of her eye she saw movement, the flickering of metal, then heard the clanking of swords, as she spun around to see Benny locking swords with one of the Spanish crew. *The Margola*'s crew moving in with swords and daggers drawn, preventing an uprising amongst the Spanish crew.

"Don't harm him! Don't harm him, Benny!" She shouted, as she sprinted towards them. Just as Benny was about to pierce the sailor's chest, Sofia's sword came down, stopping Benny's sword, shocking both men to a standstill.

"Stop! We aren't here to harm anyone!" She said, breathlessly, surges of adrenaline coursing through her veins. Both men stared at her, Benny nodding, as he lowered his sword, shouts in Spanish from the Captain still stationed at the center of the ship causing the sailor to lower and holster his sword. Hearing the commotion from the deck, Mac, Jessiah and the men made their way back on deck, arriving topside in time to see Sofia standing in between Benny and the Spanish sailor.

"What did you find?" She asked Mac, turning on her heels, walking briskly towards the center of the ship.

"Wine, some art, mostly." he answered, looking skeptically at her.

"Take a quarter of the wine, leave the rest, we're finished here!" She walked past her men, as Benny stopped and stood beside Mac and Jessiah, shrugging his shoulders. Captain Barosso stiffened his back, as Sofia walked up to him, "We will take our leave now, Captain," she said, as she bowed.

"Why did you interfere? He would have had every right to kill my man." He asked, taking a step towards her, as she straightened herself.

She raised her hand, seeing her men step towards the Spanish captain.

"I don't know, but in all the ships we've plundered, you struck me the most." She glanced over at Mac, who was paying close attention to everything she was uttering. "I have a suspicion we will be seeing one another again, so we should leave on better terms." She added, walking past him.

"You're the most interesting pirate I've crossed paths with!" He shouted. She held her hand up, acknowledging the sentiment, but not turning back.

"What was that about? Since when do we board a ship, but not take their cargo, especially a ship such as that?" Mac asked sternly, standing with arms crossed, just inside the doorway of Sofia's cabin.

"We'll need him later on, I can't explain it, but we'll need him!" She said, facing a wall of maps.

Mac stood, brooding for several minutes, before walking into the center of the room, towards Sofia and the maps she was intensely studying.

"We have a job to finish, we didn't need The *Sao Mateus'* haul but he wields influence!" She said, feeling his aggrieved gaze on the back of her head. "No need for jealously!" She added, sensing the root of his consternation.

He uncrossed his arms and walked beside her, following her gaze to the path they were on to the island of Bali. He had never seen her so laser focused on anything.

"You were right, my revenge will come after reuniting the orbs. After all, my parents died protecting them." She said, turning to Mac. He simply nodded, letting his personal feelings and protests fall by the wayside.

Much of the rest of the trip to the island of Bali went without incident, steady winds and calm seas with a few stops at foreign ports for supplies and a bit of plundering.

After months in the making, *The Margola* moored to a strip of wood paneling, meant for ships, anchored to the small island. Sofia, Mac, Hugh, Benny and Red climbed into a boat, making their way to the white sandy beach. Jessiah had a team of men at the ready to join the others, if the young Scot came for them. Sofia was struck immediately by the sheer beauty of the island, a shore of white sand and blue waters. She peered down at the crystalline waters, mesmerized by its' gentleness and mix of blues and greens, staring at the shore and wondering what awaited them. Sofia stepped onto the sand, while her men hid the boat in a large patch of green shrubbery along the shoreline. She looked up at a green, textured mountain, rising out of the lush earth, a totem of spiritual beauty.

"There!" She said, as Mac stood beside her.

"Where?" He asked. She pointed to the top of the mountain, "The Futurist we are looking for is there. Apollo said find the green mountain off the shore." Her eyes were focused on the fog-covered peek, "If I was in hiding, I'd want to make it as difficult as possible for people to find me." she said, talking to herself audibly.

"Is that the only thing you think you make difficult?" Mac shook his head and laughed, as he walked past to join the others near the brush.

She let out an audible laugh, following in joining the others.

"How far do ye think this person will be up this mountain?" Hugh asked, feeling at home in the lush greenery.

"The top, I suspect. Apollo said we would know the path of the Futurist once here." Sofia said, dodging tree limbs.

"So, we haven't the foggiest of who we are looking for or where!" Benny was not as light on foot as the others. "Ouch!" He exclaimed, hitting his head on a branch.

"Watch where you're going!" Sofia chided, as she moved with cat-like reflexes, navigating the increasingly difficult terrain. "Get down!" She yelled, hearing a snap under her feet, she dropped to the ground, as the others quickly followed. A large log whizzed past their heads, a pendulum of wood, making several passes to-and-fro until the inertia was broken by a pair of sweeping, capable, woman's hands. Sofia grabbed the log out of the air and held onto it until it stopped.

"What type of place is this?" Mac, asked rhetorically, carefully brushing dirt and leaves from his clothes.

"A place with people who don't want visitors," Sofia whispered, while standing perfectly still. Benny took a step closer and another snapping sound echoed, breaking the serenity of the jungle, forcing all four newcomers to flop to the ground, as a series of logs crisscrossed the green terrain, snapping through the air one way, then back the other way.

"I think I like this person!" Sofia exclaimed, head down as she started moving across the rich red dirt on her knees and elbows.

"You would, crazy woman!" Mac yelled, as he propelled himself, using mostly knees to pull beside her. Hugh and Benny moved across the ground, side-by-side, protecting each other's weak side, as they often did in battle. A blanket of darkness slowly covered the ground around them. Sofia and Mac stopped at the same time, both rising together, seeing no more flying logs and sensing a presence watching them. Hugh and Benny stood beside Mac, hands on their swords, eyes shifting from side to side. Sofia swung around, both hands gripping the hilt of her sword, swinging at the darkness and landing with a sharp clank! She jumped back, forcing her attacker out of the shadows, as Mac, Hugh and Benny stood with swords at the ready, shifting weight from side-to-side in hypnotic, synchronized moves. A fast-moving streak of steel and Sofia leaped back again, her long muscular legs flexing, eyes shifting in the blackness, pulse rapidly accelerating. There was a whistle and a wall of bodies, and arms flailing with swords, while shields flew into the air.

Red, stationed at the base of the hill, had heard the swordplay and ran back to *The Margola*. Jessiah, seeing the young Scot as a moving dot from the ship, led 10 men to the beach. He met Red at the base of the mountain. "Lead us to where they are!" Jessiah said, in a loud whisper.

Red didn't utter a word, sliding across the ground, as he turned around and headed back up the mountain with Jessiah and the small group of men from *The Margola*. Sofia and Mac were fighting, side-by-side, as next to them, Hugh and Benny were fighting back-to-back, all striking and blocking by senses, as light had been snuffed out.

"Captain! We are here, Captain!" Jessiah shouted, as some of the wall of fighters shifted towards him and the crew.

"Don't kill them, any of them!" Sofia shouted back, "I want them alive, all of them!" She added, breathlessly.

"Yes, Captain!" Jessiah and the men said in unison, sounding busy with their own assailants.

"We mean you no harm!" Sofia yelled, as she exchanged clanking of swords with the ghosts of darkness.

"She's Captain Sofia Bonny Rose!" Mac yelled into the void, as he fended off a series of swords. Just like that, the fighting ceased, the wall of fighters retreated.

"Captain Rose, we weren't expecting you so soon, please, you and your men follow us." The voice, silky smooth, slight with an accent Sofia couldn't place. A hand, with a long slender feminine finger inches away from Sofia's face, beckoned her to follow.

"Jed, are you here?" She asked, turning around into the black of night.

"Yes, Captain!" Came a familiar voice.

"Make sure the men stay up with us!" She commanded.

"Yes, Captain!" He answered, knowing a nod wouldn't be effective. Sofia followed the figure in front of her, hearing the crushing of leaves and shuffling of feet, as Mac, Hugh and Benny remained close to her, while Jessiah and Red were a small distance behind, bringing up the rest of the men. They walked for hours, and the darkness eased, allowing for shadows to emerge, exhaustion setting in just as the figures stopped.

"Your men will make camp and rest here with my people!" The voice commanded, firmly.

"I won't go without the men I've been traveling with." Sofia fired back, one hand on the hilt of her sword and the other touching the orb around her chest, beneath her shirt.

"Of course, they may proceed with you."

It was another couple of hours to the top of the mountain, the darkness became lighter and friendlier as the minutes passed. There was a mist gathering, swirling around their ankles, as their hosts stopped.

Sofia wiped her eyes with her shirt, covering her arm. "This is amazing!" She whispered, stupefied at the site before her, an elaborately crafted domicile, uniquely crafted for housing and religious worship alike. Mac, Hugh and Benny were equally taken with the dwelling, as Hugh and Benny, infinitely more spiritual than their counterparts, went down to their knees and bowed their heads in respect.

"I am Wayan." the figure was in full view now, a small, thin, elegantly-formed woman with black hair shaped in a bun on top of her head, eyes dark and full.

"Sofia, but you know that. How did you know I was coming?" She asked, matching Wayan's warm gaze.

"We are Futurists! We sense things, besides Apollo sent word months ago you were embarking on reuniting the orbs." She said, laughing.

"Months ago? How could that be? We set out as soon as we left him, he couldn't have possibly known…" Sofia stopped, thoughts jumbled inside her head, trying to make sense of this.

"Step inside, please," Wayan opened the door, barely tall enough for Sofia, Mac and Hugh to walk through without ducking, but Benny cleared it easily. Candles illuminated every corner of the interior, books were neatly stacked in the back of the dwelling, mats lined the edges, and a long table with short, stubby legs with cushions in place of chairs lined the center of the massive room. Wayan and her two companions gracefully sat on the cushions, crossing their legs simultaneously. Sofia nodded and plopped to the floor a little less gracefully, as she crossed her long muscular legs, shifting to find a comfortable spot. Mac's brows narrowed, as he glanced at Hugh and Benny, the floor where the cushions sat, then back at Sofia, who started laughing at the thought of her men attempting to sit on the cushions. Mac led Hugh and Benny to stand directly behind Sofia.

"I hope you don't mind," she said, addressing Wayan, gesturing at the men standing behind her.

"Not at all," Wayan laughed. "My mother was a Futurist, we were on a ship after Fury waged war, taking the orb to safety when we were attacked by a couple of the crew, loyal to Fury. My mother gave me the orb, hid me and told me not to come out, no matter what I heard. That's the last time I saw her. She sent

Marta to me." Wayan explained, pointing to the older woman on her right. "We escaped in a small boat, got to land and, with help of fellow Futurists, onto another ship bound for here. My family originates from this island." She said, exhaling, "We came back and other Futurists from neighboring islands joined us." She continued, her and Sofia's eyes meeting one another.

"My mom was…" Sofia started.

"We know who your mom was!" Wayan said, cutting Sofia off.

"I suppose you do," she simply said, not sure what to say next.

"You're going to reunite the orbs, is that right?" Wayan asked, skepticism bubbling in and undercurrent of her words.

"Yes, we have come for the orb you have so courageously hid and protected all these years, so we can reunite it with the others and bring you all out of hiding!" Sofia exclaimed, aware it must sound far-fetched to Wayan and all those Futurists who've spent much of their existence in hiding.

"We have one request, Marta and myself that is." she said, rising.

"What's that?" Sofia's brows furrowed, in anticipation.

"We come with you on your quest, we help guard the orbs until they are all reunited." She said, voice even and confident.

Sofia took in a deep breath, rose from the table, glanced back at her men, looking for some help in denying the request. Finding no articulable rational to reject the help, she nodded in acceptance.

"Shall we set sail at once?" Wayan asked, anxious to leave the small island she and the others had found both refuge and prison all these years.

"Yes, it's a long way to the colonies!" She said, the corners of her mouth curved upwards, in relief, having additional help in securing the orbs. They rendezvoused with the rest of the men of *The Margola*, somewhat shocked to find all of Wayan's group of warriors were entirely women.

"Captain!" Jessiah shouted, jumping up, a beautiful young woman sitting next to him, sharpening a rugged blade on a rock, paying Sofia no mind.

"Please, continue what it is you were doing Jed," she laughed, as he turned several shades of pink from embarrassment. "Is there a place we can grab supplies from?" Sofia asked, turning to Wayan.

"Halfway down the mountain there's a small path, which leads to a village with supplies. I'll take you there!" She was eager to oblige, the thought of escaping such a beautiful place was initially puzzling to Sophia but sensing Wayan's desperation, she realized even a beautiful prison is a prison nonetheless, binding soul and body alike.

"Stay here!" She said, turning to Mac, just audible for him to hear her.

"Where you go, so will I!" He said with conviction. She caught his gaze, knowing it was one of those times her order meant nothing to him.

"The two of you can stay," she looked over at Benny and Hugh, looking every bit as zapped of energy as she felt.

"No! We promised Apollo we wouldn't let you or the orbs out of our sight and we aim to keep that promise!" Hugh said, speaking for the duo.

"Well then, Wayan, if you'd please." She motioned her hand at the space in front of her, Wayan bowed and took the lead. Sofia rubbed her eyes thinking she was suffering from fatigue, she closed them and opened them again, staring at a fully-functioning town. Food carts lined the center of the path, locals trading and buying on local currency, as slight structures dotted the paths on both sides, including homes, medical and a make-shift jail.

"I know, I feel their presence." Sofia whispered, as Mac leaned in. Two men casually slipped behind Benny, and a small group had formed up the road.

"Keep walking, it's ok." Sofia uttered, sensing Wayan's hesitation in moving towards the men. Sofia placed her hand on the hilt of her sword, while Mac casually placed one hand on his sword and tapped the back of his head twice with his other hand, a signal he shared with everyone close to him for times such as these.

"Aye!" Hugh said, just audible enough for Mac to hear, as they were now flanked on all sides.

"Do you have the orb on you?" Sofia asked Wayan in a whisper.

"No, it's with Marta, I don't take it into town" she whispered back.

The townspeople scattered, leaving Sofia, her men, Wayan and the would-be assassins. There was no more illusion of surprise, the men were closing in from all sides.

"Now!" She commanded.

Hugh and Benny spun off their heels, facing men from behind and at each of their sides, swords wildly flying from back to side and back again. Their steps were synchronized as a rhythmic dance, both sensing the others' movements, defending the others' weaker side, moving as one. Sofia's concern for Wayan quickly eased, as the island warrior exhibited her skills, she stabbed one and slashed another, then moving onto a third before Sofia was able to glance back in her direction. A loud grunt came from behind, she knew that sound and knew whom it came out of, she took a deep breath, slashing two men in front of her and another to her side before spinning around to find Mac bleeding from a gash which extended from his shoulder blade to his elbow.

"I'm all right!" He managed, as he flung his sword wildly with one hand, fending off two attackers, Benny altering positions to help take on a couple attackers who smelled blood in the air. Rage sparked and ran through Sofia like a live wire, adrenaline coursing through her muscles giving her the strength of two men! She spun back and forth, a killing machine, with no want, no patience and no time for sword play, finished with this group of would-be's, as blood spewed from one man, then from another and another. Moments later, the fighting ceased, and the island's people slowly emerged, clapping for the victorious. Sofia, covered in blood, although none her own, with muscles involuntarily convulsing, and hands shaking with leftover adrenaline, the high quickly receding, as she tended to Mac's gaping wound. She ripped the bottom of her shirt into hefty strips, wrapping the entire arm, as blood steadily ran.

"I'm fine," he said, looking for the dagger he dropped.

"We need to get you back onto *The Margola*," there was a noticeable panic in Sofia's voice, something none of her men were used to hearing from her.

"We have a medicine doctor on the island, she's close." Wayan said, altering her course and quickening her steps. Hugh and Benny propped Mac up, by the underside of his shoulders, blood still seeping and Mac losing strength with every step. They came to the door of a small hut, and Wayan opened the door and motioned for the group to step inside.

"This is our Shaman, medical healer." Wayan said, by way of introducing a small, seemingly frail, older woman with white, strangely hair. Wayan and the woman spoke in a foreign language, a quick exchange, as the healer pointed to Mac, leading Hugh and Benny to deposit him on a rug-covered table. She prayed in chants, sprinkling a liquid over the wound, sewed the skin together and ran stones up and down his arm, as he fell peacefully, painlessly asleep. The healer slowly walked over to Sofia, sitting on a pillow, she stayed perfectly still as the old woman gently touched her forehead with the stones. She instantly relaxed, adrenaline gone from her body, anxiety and the tension from the past few hours zapped.

"Thank you," Sofia smiled at the healer, extending her long arms, gently squeezing the old woman's hands. The healer lightly squeezed her hands in return, creases of her small, wrinkled mouth slowly turning upwards.

"Who were those men?" Sofia asked Wayan, keeping her voice low.

"I've never seen any of them before." she responded with her head down, staring at the floorboards.

"You knew we were walking into a trap!" Sofia's eyes narrowed, fixated on the back of Wayan's head, as she refused to look up.

"I didn't have a choice." she whispered, "Fury's men found our stronghold, days before you arrived. Some men took her on a ship, leaving these men to ambush you." Wayan picked her head up slightly, avoiding any eye contact with Sofia.

"Took who?" Sofia asked.

"My sister, Made."

"Do they have the orb?" Sofia asked, dispassionately.

"No," she said simply, slightly shaking her head, "they took my sister because I wouldn't give up the orb." She added, looking up at Sofia.

"What were you going to do if we were killed?" She asked Wayan, crouching down beside her.

"Your reputation precedes you!" Her response surprised Sofia.

"Reputation?" Sofia questioned, rising to her full height.

"Your skills are well known, exploits legendary," Wayan smiled, sensing a break in Sofia's armor. Sofia took in a large sum of air, slowing exhaling in reflective acquiescence of the situation before them. Fury, a true maniacal mastermind, had been steps and oceans ahead of her for longer than she knew of his existence. It was well into the dark of night before Mac was well enough to head back to rendezvous with the men of *The Margola*. They bid their hostess and healer farewell, Sofia slipping several gold coins into her hands, as the group slipped out into the night.

"Jed, is that you?" She asked, making out the familiar silhouette from an unusually luminescent moonbeam.

"Aye, Captain, I was getting worried something had happened." He uttered, clearing his throat.

She made a gurgling sound in her throat, catching Wayan's glance, "We need to get back to the ship. Are the men ready?" She asked.

"Aye, they are in the clearing with the women just as when ye left." He assured, turning around once Sofia was in his full view.

❈ ❈ ❈

The sun was making its' way up to the horizon once they reached *The Margola*.

"It's nice to see you Captain!"

"It's nice to be seen, Mr. Longfellow!" Sofia's mood lightened instantly at the sight and sounds of the poet's soft voice. Wayan stood at the top of the gangplank, Marta by her side, both uneasy, unsure what to do next. Sofia glanced in their direction, motioning them aboard. Wayan nodded, walking slowly onto *The Margola*, she walked up to Sofia, "This belongs in your possession." She said, handing Sofia the orb her and her people had protected for years.

"We'll get your sister back!" Sofia assured her, hands delicately plucking the orb from Wayan.

Chapter 25

Mac was standing by the railing, soaking up some much-needed warmth.

"You scared me," Sofia informed him, leaning over the railing next to him.

"Serves ya right, now you know how it feels every time you try and get yourself killed!" He started laughing, head and wound aching from the vibrations. "Ouch!" He gently touched around the stitches, with his arm propped in a sling from a soft cloth. It had been a couple of days since they set sail and his first day up and about.

"If Wayan didn't take us directly to the medicine woman, you wouldn't have made it!" She informed him.

"I don't remember much of the medicine woman, where we were or how we got there, come to think of it," he was scratching his head with his good arm, trying to recall something from the time after he was injured.

"Don't scare me like that again!" She chided, "Brush up on your fighting skills!" She commanded, as she walked away from him. He turned his head, watching her walk to her cabin.

"You know it's strange with the two of you," Jessiah stated, walking up after Sofia had left, "She was more worried than I've ever seen when you were hurt!"

Mac chuckled at the thought, "Wish I was conscious enough to have seen that." His gaze trailed off into the horizon, "It's me who worries and shows my care for her, while she puts herself in harm's way." He continued, shifting his gaze to catch Jessiah's reaction.

"Aye, well what did ya expect when you fell for a woman Captain?" Jessiah said, matter of factly.

"Right now, the only thing that matters is reuniting the orbs and getting Fury. None of us are safe until then." Mac said, rubbing his arm.

"Aye!" Jessiah agreed, nodding his head, coming back to the dangerous realities befalling them, as he left Mac to his sunbathing. Months went by with a couple of minor stops for supplies, Sofia leading small groups into town, the second orb remaining in Wayan's care, on board *The Margola*. Sofia never once removed her orb for anything other than the occasional adjustment or rewrapping of the material sling. She knew after Bali, Fury had international reach, with loyalists throughout land and sea. The quicker they could reach the colony of New York, and find the third orb, the sooner she could go after Fury.

They landed in the colony of New York, a bustling new world, a hotbed of trade and life. At Jessiah's insistence, Sofia allowed the crew to venture onto land, in groups, leaving men to guard *The Margola* at all times. Sofia carried both orbs safely under her shirt, in the same material she'd had the first orb wrapped in since seeing Apollo. Sofia, Wayan, Mac, Hugh and Benny walked around the harbor, marveling at the people and structures. This was a much larger place then Bali Sofia had no idea where to look or whom to look for.

Mac, having been forced into weeks of convalescence thanks to his captain, was now fully recovered and marveling at the sights and sounds of the new world. There was a surprising sophistication to the colony, he thought, for a place too far from the epicenter of the world. Jessiah requested permission to take the crew into town, leaving Marta to watch over the orb and Mr. Longfellow to guard the ship for a few hours. Sofia granted his request, feeling the crew might be close to mutiny following the months at sea.

"Made?" Wayan suddenly cried out, darting down a cobbled-stone street behind some buildings.

"It has to be a trap!" Sofia called out, glancing behind her, seeing Mac, Hugh and Benny rushing to catch up.

Sofia rounded the corner behind the buildings at her full running speed but came to a screeching halt, seeing Wayan standing perfectly still. Hearing her men close behind, Sofia held up her hand as she pulled her sword from its sheath, feverishly searching for signs of their adversaries. Hugh, Benny and Mac rounded the corner, and Hugh, slightly ahead of the other two, was first to see Sofia's signal and pulled his sword before coming to a complete stop. The other two followed within seconds, landing within feet of Sofia.

"Not again!" Sofia uttered, barely audible; eyeing a young girl with a dirk against her throat; thrusted out into the middle of the cobblestone street. Her captor, a tall man with dark, wavy hair, tied neatly with a ribbon; his clothes curiously clean, pressed and not common amongst the Fury loyalists.

"Enter scary men with swords surrounding us…" She said, rolling her eyes, disappointed with the redundancy of ambushes. "Would it kill him for some originality?" She said out loud, more than a hint of sarcasm billowing in her voice.

"I'd really like to not get wounded or killed in this latest skirmish of yours, Sofia, if you don't mind." Mac said sardonically.

"Well, then, I suggest you step up your fighting skills!" She mused.

He chuckled at her response, allowing her the last word; he enjoyed the challenge and knew she wasn't completely wrong.

"Made!" Wayan cried out, taking several hurried steps towards her sister.

"Get back or she dies right here!" The man shouted. Wayan stopped, holding her free hand up and lowering her other hand, still clutching the sword.

"Ok, please don't hurt her." Wayan urged, her voice noticeably trembling.

"What is it you want?" Sofia asked, calm and unwavering.

"You and your men, dead!" He announced. Men began surrounding them, blocking them in from behind and filling the empty cobblestoned street with menacing, armed bodies.

"Hmm, let me think," she looked up briefly, smiling wryly, "No that's not going to work!" She said, eyes narrowing.

"Kill them!" The man yelled, swiftly backing up with his dagger at Made's throat, dragging her as she cried. The men organized themselves in rows of fighting teams; each team consisting of 10 to 15 men, surrounding Sofia, Mac, Hugh and Benny, as Wayan went after her sister and her captor. The first team of 10 men rushed in, they were organized and most fair to good with a sword, Sofia; misjudged as the weakest link of the group dispensed her one foe within minutes, turning on heel as soon as she pulled her sword from the new corpse. There were three men assigned to each of her crew, so she sprang up in the middle of Mac and Benny, stabbing one with her dagger and the other her sword.

"That was easy enough!" She said, delighted with herself and feeling rather confident, as she pushed the second man backwards. A loud whistling noise signaled the second group of men, this one consisting of 12 men and three sent to lock swords with Sofia.

"They must have judged you as a menace with a sword!" Mac said, catching his breath, as he ducked, thrusting his sword in a man's gut.

"They'd be right!" She called back, sweeping the legs out from one of the men, stabbing him with her dagger, as soon as he hit the ground, while thrusting her sword behind her and into the man foolish enough to try and take her from behind. Sofia, Mac, Hugh and Benny stood side-by-side and back-to-back; having defeated the second round of men.

"They're changing their strategy of attack!" Sofia uttered, watching men flood into the street from the shadows of the surrounding buildings.

"Aye, ye keep killing their men!" Hugh said, adding some much-needed levity. Sofia, heartbeat accelerating, shifted her stance, eyes focused on the flood of men coming towards them.

Several shots rang out and the smell of gun powder permeated the air. Sofia glanced up, seeing movement on the roofs of the buildings, as men fell dead in front of her, with arrows through their backs. Another whistle sparked another surge of attack, as Sofia and her men fought for their lives against the seemingly endless scores of attackers. Sofia, senses hyper-focused on keeping her men and herself alive, hadn't seen the scores of fighters surrounding the enemy; making it a much more equitable skirmish.

※ ※ ※

Chasing after her sister and her sister's captor led Wayan inside one of the buildings, lost in a web of candlelit rooms. She walked through the rooms, occasionally marking the wood with her sword. There was an eerie quiet, enough that she could hear the pounding of her own heart, as she walked into the largest room in the building.

"Where's the orb?" Her sister's captor asked, in a commanding voice.

"Safe!" Wayan replied, voice erupting with confidence and conviction.

"You'll bring it to me if you want your sister back with her head attached!" The man said, sternly. Made started crying again, her small frame convulsing from the shock and tears; she was 14 years old and had just entered the same training Wayan completed, before becoming the protector of the orb, so she wasn't able to assist in her own rescue.

Wayan put that fact into her quick mental calculation as to what her next steps should be.

"Ok," she said, resignation in her voice, hoping to sound believable, "I will get it and bring it to you, as long as you don't harm my sister!"

The man's brows arched in pensive reflection, then his eyes narrowed in a menacing gaze, sending chills down Wayan's back. "You have one hour, if you are one minute late, she dies, and if you bring anyone back through those doors, she dies!" He tightened his grip on Made's throat, making her gasp audibly.

Wayan nodded in understanding, "I'll be back within the hour, not a minute later and alone!" She said, turning on her heel, quickly following the marks she created back to the outside street. Wayan made it back to find Sofia, as the last of the foe's fell where they stood. "I found her. A man has her in the far building over there." She pointed to the largest building at the end of the street.

"Who is he?" Sofia questioned, catching her breath, covered in dead men's blood.

"I can answer that!" A tall figure came forward, wearing a hood.

"Thank you for your help, if it wasn't for you and your men we would have been in real trouble." Sofia confided, "Now who are you?"

"Lady Robynette Hillshire, at your service Captain Rose, I go by Robyn" she removed her hood, revealing her reddish-brown curls, hanging down around her face onto her shoulders, a few inches shorter than Sofia but a formidable figure. She held her bow in her hand and a sack of arrows across her shoulder. "My group of men and women have been caring for the orb for the past couple of years after The Futurist was kidnapped and killed by Fury's men in another colony. She had hidden it, telling only Apollo it's whereabouts, so when he got word that she was killed, he sent word to me." She explained with a warm and gracious smile. "We are sure happy you've come, so we can go back home and come out of hiding, although I think I'll keep the bow!" The corners of her mouth curled upwards, as her eyes reflected her mischievous personality.

"Oh, I like her!" Sofia said out loud, turning to Mac.

"Wonderful, another you in this world! That's what we all need!" Mac said, raising his hands in the air in defeat, as there was a wave of chuckling and quiet laughter. Wayan stood next to Sofia, impatiently tapping her foot. "Where's the orb?" Sofia asked, turning the tide of the conversation back to their reality.

"The orb is with us, safe, and I'll transfer it to you once you're ready to board your ship. Now, as for the man, he is one of Fury's top lieutenants, an evil man, goes by Maddox." Robyn said.

"He doesn't look like the usual Fury devotee." Sofia commented, recalling his clothes and sight of his hair.

"No, he doesn't!" Wayan agreed.

"That's because he's not!" Robyn took a step towards Wayan.

"He was part of the crown, born to a wealthy, political family; Fury kidnapped him as a child, and he ended up raising him as his own.

As much as Fury is capable of loving another human." She explained.

"He wants the orb within this hour or he'll kill her!" Wayan said, trying to subdue the panic rising within her.

"The girl, she's your sister?" Robyn asked. Wayan nodded, contorting her body, half in the conversation and half pulling towards the building. "He was sent here to prevent us from coming out of hiding. Fury knows he'll never get all the orbs. He fears you Sofia!" She said, turning to Sofia in admiration.

"He's never come across me, how could a pirate with his reputation be scared of me?" She asked, her eyes meeting Robyn's.

"You're the chosen one, you'll be his end and he very well knows it!" She said, moving onto the business of rescuing Wayan's sister. "There's a way into the building, a back way, but we'll have to fight some of his men to get there, if you're up for it!" She said, turning to Sofia.

"There isn't a fight I'm not up for!" Sofia responded, having a newly-found reputation to live up too.

"We can attest to that!" Came a chorus of voices. Sofia shot a stern glance at her men.

"Wayan, you go in just the way you did before. We'll be there to back you up!" Robyn said, following Wayan's eyes to Sofia. Sofia nodded and Wayan ran at full tilt, towards the door she followed her sister and Maddox through.

They moved quickly, following Robyn and a group of her men and women fighters, weaving in and out of alleys to an adjoining building.

"Apollo told me about this passage way; it will allow us to sneak into the building without any of Maddox's men being the wiser." She smiled, slyly.

"I wonder where Jessiah and my crew are." Sofia said, thinking out loud.

"He would have come running if he had any inkling or heard the commotion." Mac insisted.

Just then, a rock fell off the roof. "Red?" Sofia whispered in disbelief, as they were quickly approaching the door to the building. The young Scot tactfully climbed down to the ground, landing without a sound.

"What are you doing here?" Sofia yelled in a whisper through gritted teeth, grabbing his arm.

"Jessiah sent me! He had me keep watch on you and the guys, I saw ye run, and heard the shots; saw the men on the roof, so I went into town to tell him. Took me a bit to track them."

"Where are Jed and the men?" Sofia asked, letting the boy's arm go.

"They went to secure the ship, Captain." He uttered, leaning in close to her, hoping she caught his meaning. She nodded, acknowledging she got his meaning and the decision was a good one.

"Go back to *The Margola*!" Sofia commanded, glancing over to Robyn, who was now standing with her hand on the door handle.

"We won't be long, so let Jed know we are about to rescue Wayan's sister and we need to set sail as soon as we board." She whispered, turning her body and focus back to the mission. Red was gone before Robyn opened the door. She led them through a long rectangular room into a narrow hallway, where they moved one-by-one, in rhythmic unison and into another room.

"It's over here!" She motioned for Sofia, as she pried open a wooden slab, revealing a dark, narrow tunnel.

"And, of course, this was made for short people—" Sofia took a deep breath, as if she was diving into the sea.

"She's got a touch of claustrophobia." Mac announced in a hushed voice, immediately feeling the sharp end of Sofia's dagger just below his stomach. The tunnel was no more than an eighth of a mile but between the rich darkness, cramped space and unexpected drops and turns, Sofia was a slight shade of blueish green once Robyn opened the door on the other side.

"I'm not doing that again!" Sofia muttered, bending over, hands fixed on her knees. Mac gently placed his hand on her back, and Sofia sprung up, the point of her dagger just below his chin.

"You mention this to Jed or any of the men and I'll slit your throat!" She warned. It was one thing to show compassion and empathy, as Sofia believed it exhibited strength, but to have an irrational fear of enclosed spaces was clearly a weakness.

"Aye Captain, I've known for years of your—" he made a noise in his throat, as she pushed the dagger up to his skin, "And I haven't said a word to a living soul." He exhaled in relief, as soon as she pulled her dagger away.

Robyn placed her finger to her lips, as she led the group to the opposite side of the large room. They could hear a man's voice coming from the next room, and although slightly muffled, they knew it was Maddox. There was the occasional vibration in the floor from his men walking the rooms and hallways. Robyn tapped Sofia on the shoulder, pointing to a missing brick that allowed Robyn to shoot her bow into the next room. She slowly removed an arrow from her bag, spotted Maddox, lined up her shot and held her position. Sofia nodded, signaling Mac, Hugh and Benny to follow her. This would be a perfect time to have Red, she thought, as she poked her head out into the dark hallway. There were at least six men lingering at the end of it. She heard Wayan telling Maddox she had the orb, stalling until Robyn and Sofia got into position.

Sofia held her hand up, giving Robyn the go-ahead, as Sofia, Mac, Hugh and Benny charged down the hall, swords blazing. While Robyn shot Maddox through the shoulder, the rest of the men and women secured Made and gave chase to a wounded Maddox.

Maddox successfully evaded capture, his protection team dead, and Made happily back with her sister. Robyn's fighters stayed in the area of the buildings, as Sofia, her men, and Made walked down to the port. Wayan had gone ahead, leaving her sister in the safe hands of Sofia. Several minutes after they reached the port, they spotted Wayan talking with a couple of men and a woman. She quickly went to them.

"Thank you!" Wayan said, graciously bowing to Robyn and her band of fighters. "Captain, I've arranged passage for Made back to Bali, they are long trusted friends." She reached out and grabbed her sister's hand.

"Why not escort her back to Bali?" Sofia asked, one brow arched in curiosity.

"I owe you a debt." She said simply, eyes meeting Sofia's, "I will see the day you destroy Fury." She turned on heel, sister in tow towards the waiting ship.

"Your people are loyal, Captain Rose!" Robyn stated.

"She doesn't belong to me, she's a warrior with a sense of duty!" Sofia said.

"That's where you're wrong, Captain Rose, she's a Futurist; you are our leader!" She took the lead, long, confident strides.

"You aren't much older than myself, it isn't possible you knew my parents, is it?" Sofia stopped, all the men behind her stopped; Robyn turned facing her, "I did know them. Your mother was my mother's sister!" Her eyes softened, a single tear trickled down her cheek.

"What?" Sofia turned ghostly white, "You're my—"

"Cousin!" Robyn announced. "You didn't notice the family resemblance?" She added.

"Your parents...my aunt and uncle?" Sofia asked, too shocked for complete thoughts.

"In hiding, I don't know where." When your parents and the other Futurists decided it was best to split the orbs and send us into hiding, so my parents sent my brother and I onto a ship to the colonies to live with friends, since Fury was trying to track them down. We've had no word from them. Apollo is hopeful once you kill Fury and we are all able to come out of hiding we can be reunited." Robyn's mouth curled upwards, "Go, free us, cousin."

Robyn removed the orb from a false compartment on the bottom of her quiver and handed it to Sofia. Sofia took it, gave a slight nod and quickly made her way up the gangplank to *The Margola*.

"I have family." Sofia thought, as she sat reflecting on a rather lonely childhood, longing for a normal childhood with parents, grandparents, aunts, uncles, and cousins. Her emotions were at war, despair over a lifetime of loss, contentment over finding a living relative on her mother's side and intense rage for the man at the root of it all!

Chapter 26

"This is Judgement Day." Sofia thought, as she stood looking out at the horizon, sun barely showing itself, the water as still as glass, the calm before the storm and she was the storm! This was the reckoning, Fury's reckoning, retribution for all done to her family, to The Futurists, for the disruption, the death, all of it! She snuck off the ship, armed with her sword, her mother's dagger, two guns and extra powder inside her boot.

There was rumor of a secret passageway between a large rock, where they were moored and the back of No Name Island. Sofia found it! She climbed onto the rock and made her way to a small crevice, just large enough for her to push herself down into. It was a strip of wet sand, but the water was blocked by some abnormal volcanic spew, about 15 feet to another small opening onto the rocky backside of No Name.

❈ ❈ ❈

"She's gone!" Mac stormed out of Sofia's cabin, a murderous look in his eyes.

"The Captain?" Jessiah asked, shocked.

"Aye!" Mac glanced his way, brows narrowed in a mix of disgust and contempt, feeling he could snap her neck if she were in front of him.

"Let's go!" He commanded, looking straight ahead at the island.

"Did you two know?" He asked, stepping up just inches from Hugh's nose.

"Do ye not think we wouldn't have gone with her if we could'na stop her? Apollo will have our heads if anything happens to her!"

Mac was seldom forceful. It was Sofia who was lightning in a bottle but Mac was a bomb waiting for the right time to explode and only Sofia could ignite that fuse. He held Hugh's gaze before nodding in agreement, he knew the two of them would have gone with her or would have, at the very least, followed closely behind.

"Red! Red!" Mac screamed, scanning the deck for the young red-headed Scot.

"Yes, sir!" The boy jumped down from the mast, keeping watch for movement on the island.

"Did you see the Captain from up there?" Mac asked, walking towards the boy.

"No, sir! Haven't seen any movement at all."

Mac, stepped up to the boy, hands flexibly balled into fists. "How is it you didn't see your Captain step off this ship and saw no sign of her make her way onto that island, tell me that!"

Red, took a step back, lip quivering, not knowing how to respond.

"You know the Captain is clever." Jessiah said, stepping in the middle of the young Scot and Mac's balled-up fists. "If she didn't want anyone to know she was slipping off this ship, you know better than anyone here she would make sure not to be seen!"

Mac took a deep breath, slowly exhaling, letting his hands relax as he gave a slight nod to Jessiah. "Let's go find her!" He said, as he turned on heel, "Jessiah, you, Hugh and Benny with me, Red you're coming too! We'll need your tracking skills. The rest of you…" He raised his voice, stepping more to the middle of the deck, "Once we locate the Captain, Red will come to lead you to where we are. Does everyone understand?" He looked around, seeing the nods and hearing the unsynchronized but unison "ayes."

"Mr. Longfellow! Where is Mr. Longfellow?" Mac was again searching the deck for the small poet.

"Here, sir!" Came a small but confident voice, making his way through the crowd of men.

"Mr. Longfellow, will you please help ready these men for battle, Wayan and Marta hold back a few men to help you guard the ship!" Mac hadn't waited for a response, but turned on his heel, as he caught Red's gaze and motioned for him to join.

"Yes, sir, I will, sir!" Mr. Longfellow assured Mac, as he watched the small group head through the crowd of men on deck towards the gangplank.

❋ ❋ ❋

Sofia crouched down behind a series of small shrubbery, images of a dagger to her throat came to her in vivid clarity, as she stared at a path, looking similar to the one she was forced down when she was taken by Fury's men, while saving young Toby on Porcus. A slight shiver went through her, flashbacks taking her back all those months to the other island.

Lost in her own cobweb of emotions and shelved memories; she never heard the group behind her, as a hand covered her mouth, spinning her around.

"Sh…!" Mac said, sternly.

"What are you doing here?" She hissed, glancing over to the clearing and back towards him.

"What am I doing here? What am I doing here?" He hissed through clenched teeth, just inches away from her face. "You actually think you can take down the most ruthless pirate in our history by yourself?"

Sofia glared back over to the clearing, scanning again for a posted lookout, she rose, slightly grabbing Mac by the arm and pulling him behind a large tree. "I will be the one who kills him!" She said, stoned faced, eyes burning with an intensity Mac had not seen before.

"You shouldn't have left the ship without us!" He barked back, leaning into her, barely an inch taller than her. He held her murderous gaze as her brows softened.

"I will be the one to kill Fury!" She uttered again, pursing her lips.

"Nobody else cares who kills him, as long as he dies on this day! You'll be the one to rid the earth of the devil!" He reassured her, his temper easing.

"I hate to break up this latest argument," Benny started, "we have movement!" He conveyed, crouching behind the same shrubbery Sofia had been. Sofia and Mac went down to their knees and crawled over to the brush next to Benny. Hugh and Jessiah were several feet to their right, Hugh had one eye closed and the other eye intensely monitoring a young, gangly redheaded Scot, moving through the brush, weaving in and out of the trees. Sofia's eyebrows arched, as she caught glimpses of the enemy coming out of the structures. Fury was expecting them, he knew she would come for the last orb, he knew she would come for him.

"You have a plan, I suspect," Mac whispered, turning his head slightly to see her in deep thought.

"He brought in reinforcements." she whispered, hanging her head in momentary defeat.

In this very moment, Mac couldn't find his usual empathy for her, as he was irritated, annoyed by her antics, her inability to think things through before taking action, while her crew was left to clean up the mess left in her wake. She sprung up, crouching down on her muscular legs, rocking back on her heels, long hair flowing, spirit and mind of a hunter alive in her eyes.

"Where are you going?" Mac asked, tersely.

She pointed down to where the young Scot was currently nesting. "Stay here until I signal for you!" She glanced from Mac, to Hugh, to Benny, to Jessiah, then back to Mac, looking for signs of understanding and agreement.

"Aye Captain!" A soft chorus from three of them.

"And you?" She asked scornfully, raising her whispered voice.

Mac caught her contemptuous gaze, "Aye," he managed, barely audible, as he lowered his eyes.

"Good!" She exclaimed, excitedly, as she darted forward, moving swiftly across the soft dirt, moving from tree-to-tree and crawling on hands and knees through the brush, mindful of the multiplying eyes, as day broke.

"What in the world is she doing?" Jessiah asked, as he tracked her moves.

"Going to get herself killed!" Mac sighed heavily, as he shook his head.

Chapter 27

Sofia jumped into a dried-up ravine bed, yards from Red. He turned around, startled, dagger in his hand. Sofia put her finger up to her lips and grabbed the boy's arm, pulling him down into a crouching position with her.

"Captain!" Red exclaimed, not able to contain his exuberance.

"Sh!" She admonished, putting her finger back to her lips for added emphasis. "I'm going to follow this path around to the backside to sneak up on Fury, kill him and get the orb before his men are the wiser. You keep an eye out and signal for the others, if things don't go as planned." She explained, calmly.

Red's brows narrowed, as he searched for the proper response, too afraid to tell her she was out of her mind. "Do ya think that's the wisest plan?" He asked, pushing himself back. "I mean, there are a lot of men and the tales of Fury say he's no ordinary pirate." He added, pushing back further, trying to avoid her reach.

Sofia inhaled and exhaled slowly, "Do as your Captain tells you." She scolded, "He's only a man!" She whispered, leaning closer to him, corners of her mouth turned upwards.

"Aye Captain," the ginger Scot replied, holding Sofia's gaze in admiration. She peered over the ledge of the ravine, not seeing a soul in sight, she sprang up and used the cover of the trees as she moved, circling the small island, and making her way to the far side of the clearing.

"The only chance we have is to go back, get the men from the ship and hope she hasn't been spotted before we return!" Mac said in a feeble attempt to whisper, still keeping low as they watched for movement several yards away.

"I'll go, I'll bring them back!" Jessiah volunteered, waiting for Mac's approval.

Mac nodded and Jessiah was off, racing against a dark force of nature and his Captain's impetuous moves.

❈ ❈ ❈

Jessiah reached *The Margola* within the hour, heart racing and at a loss of breath, once he crossed the gangplank, it took him several minutes to gather himself.

"Are you quite all right, Jessiah, my boy?" Mr. Longfellow said, gently touching Jessiah's shoulder in genuine concern.

Jessiah nodded, laboring to catch his breath. "I need the men, are they ready for battle?" He managed to say in-between wheezing and occasionally coughing.

Mr. Longfellow put his fingers up to his mouth and made some sort of loud whistling noise, sending a stampede of men to the center of the deck. "Ready for battle, sir!" Mr. Longfellow said, beaming with pride.

"Is this the same crew we left just hours ago? My word, you are an absolute wonder, Mr. Longfellow!" Jessiah gushed, breath returning, as he admired the crew standing at attention in lines, as well groomed as any pirate, armed and ready for battle.

Momentarily mesmerized by the sight of the crew looking rather organized and like a real fighting unit he snapped back to the moment, "Let's go!" He ordered, leading the men over the gangplank. "Take good care of the ship, Mr. Longfellow!"

"Aye, will do!" Mr. Longfellow returned, proudly using the pirate's term for the very first time and feeling a sense of belonging to *The Margola*. For the first time, believing the pirate's life just might be for him.

❈ ❈ ❈

"Ship, Ship!" A man called out from *The Margola*'s crow's nest.

Mr. Longfellow ran to the side to see two healthy-looking ships rounding the bend in their direction. Wayan and Marta took their positions in the center of the deck, swords out, battle-ready.

"Apollo, it's Apollo!" The man from the crow's nest called out, a mix of excitement and relief in his voice.

"Apollo?" Wayan uttered, flabbergasted. She climbed halfway up the mast, until she was able to see the large black flag with a wild bird, the swallow in white, Apollo's own symbol of freedom and strength.

A more striking flag there was not, she thought, as tears welled up in the corners of her eyes. She had not seen Apollo since he entrusted her mother with the orb. It wasn't long before Apollo and his men landed on the deck of *The Margola*, other men coming over the gangplank by the dozens.

"Apollo, your reputation precedes you, I am honored to make your acquaintance, I am Mr. Longfellow!" The poet turned pirate, bowed, noticeably shaking with nerves. Everyone knew the legend of Black Fury but Apollo; he was folklore and Mr. Longfellow was a student of romanticism.

The corners of Apollo's mouth turned upwards as he returned the small man's bow. "I can honestly say I've never before had such a greeting after boarding a ship." He said, glancing in Ishmael's direction after hearing him chuckle. "Wayan, you're grown!" Apollo said, noticing Wayan standing off to the side, several feet away from where he was standing.

"Yes, the last time you saw me I was just a child." she announced, standing straight as she could.

"Thank you for keeping the orb safe all these years. Your mom would have been proud," he added, nodding in her direction. "You and Marta come with me. Your skills will be welcomed!" He commanded, "You, you and the 6 of you," He pointed to several men, towards the front of the crowd. "Stay here with Mr. Longfellow and guard the ship!" He turned his attention to Mr. Longfellow, who was at least a foot shorter than the towering black ghost.

"Captain Rose is on the island—." Mr. Longfellow started.

"Hunting the infamous Black Fury." Apollo finished his sentence. His eyes narrowed, as he turned in the direction of the island. He nodded in Ishmael's direction and without a word spoken, Apollo tipped his hat to Mr. Longfellow and made his way over the gangplank, Ishmael at his side and hundreds of men following in lockstep.

※ ※ ※

Mac, Jessiah, Hugh and Benny followed the path taken by Red then Sofia, and they made it to the dried ravine bed, throwing pebbles at the young Scot, getting his attention before jumping down next to him.

"She's down there." he pointed to the structures at the end of the clearing.

Mac muttered quite a few things under his breath, as he peered over the edge, spotting lots of movement in that general direction. "You stay here until we come for you!" Mac ordered, sternly. He held up his hand, eyes fixed on the structures and gave a slight wave, signaling it was time to move. As Mac, Jessiah, Benny and Hugh started moving in around the field, towards the structures, there was a loud shout from just outside the camp. Dozens and dozens of Fury's men emerged, seemingly out of nowhere. Mac froze in his tracks, sensing they were being watched. Men came from behind them shouting, nothing discernible, wielding swords, daggers and some with primitive hatchets.

Mac, Jessiah, Hugh and Benny prepared for battle, as a group soon spotted them. They were prepared to run in as many as they could before they were overrun. Fury's men far outnumbered their small gang of four.

"If this be the end of us, let's give it our all." Mac drew his sword.

"Aye." The other three swiftly drew their swords as well.

Before they could engage, familiar faces rushed from the brush and trees, men from The *Redemption* formed a perimeter around Mac and his men, facing the onslaught of Fury's loyalists.

❈ ❈ ❈

Sofia glanced toward the commotion. Apollo's men were locked in battle with Fury's. She seized the momentary chaos, snuck into Fury's dwelling and began rummaging through piles of items, no doubt from years of plundering ships.

"There ye be girl!" A large, baritone voice boomed from the doorway, "Looking for this, are ye?"

Sofia spun around, heart racing like a dozen horses, the infamous Black Fury was several inches taller than even she imagined. He was a head taller and about a foot wider, broad shoulders with an even broader midsection. His legs were like tree trunks. A long, straggly beard, mostly gray, housing remnants of his iconic black hair, occasionally intertwining the matted mess hanging from his chin.

He had his hand out, cupped, shielding something, and he laughed sadistically, as he unfurled his wide fingers. The orb seemed small sitting in the palm of his massive hand. Her eyes narrowed as she pulled her sword from its sheath, and it vibrated for several seconds on Sofia's hip, from the force of the sword's removal.

"Ye think ye be a match for me, girl? I've run-in more men in my time than ye can count!" He gave a brief laugh, followed by the most hideous snorting sound she had ever heard, as he tucked the orb into the front pocket of his overcoat.

"I'm not only a match, I'm far superior to the likes of you!" Sofia exclaimed, a mix of adrenaline and courage coursing through her veins. Fury's forehead creased in anger; his eyes narrowed, as his massive body moved side to side. Sofia stood steadfast, eyes following every move, no matter how slight, he was making; sticking to her plan of forcing him to attack first.

"Are you scared of a woman? Do I frighten you?" She taunted, hoping to send him into the same frenzy she used on his brother to seize the tactical advantage. "I'm double the swordsman you are!" She uttered, grinning, even as her heart was now pounding with such ferocity it was ringing in her ears.

The infamous pirate made sounds in his throat, beads of sweat streaming down his face, as his fist tightened around his sword and his other fist balled in sheer anger. She fought her instinct to take a step backwards, readying herself for what was to come.

"You're no match for me!" She said again, calm and confident, rocking on her heels. There was little warning, and Fury charged at her, yielding his sword with such brute strength it sent shock waves through her as she blocked his blow. She continued to block his blows, both hands clutching her sword, knowing she had to get out from under the defensive position, she spun around, as he pulled his sword to strike again. She held his menacing gaze, buying a brief moment of refuge from the unrelenting attack, as she felt streams of liquid flow from down her back. His blade caught her inches from the back of her neck, tearing shirt and skin in one sweeping blow. She felt nothing but focus, fortunate her shirt bestowed her some protection. He lunged at her again and again and again, proving himself more formidable than legend and folklore. There was a pattern, a rhythm to his attack, she thought, as she fended off his advances. She needed to force him out of his pattern, force his rhythm off! When she entered the room and started rummaging through the piles, she noticed a desk housing more items and bottles of spirits, not able to turn around, she backed up a couple of steps after each charge of the sword, taking her time so he wouldn't catch on. Her arms ached, the wound was seeping blood at a steady pace and she wasn't sure how much longer she could take such a punishing offense when her heel brushed backwards into a leg of the desk.

"Is that all you have?" She asked, impudently, hoping that would encourage him to try and end her. He pulled the sword back, mustering all the strength he had left, as Sofia ducked backwards, beneath the desk. Bottles of rum and spirits flew across the room, as other items came crashing all around. Without hesitation, Sofia stabbed Fury through one of his tree-trunk legs and flew out from the other side of the desk. He let out an ear-piercing howl, before turning on his heel, blood gushing through his pants, from the stab wound.

He stumbled towards her, muttering unintelligibly, sword flying back and forth in resentment and hostility. Suddenly the world around her appeared out of focus, she blinked multiple times in rapid succession, knowing this isn't the time for poor sight. She realized she was losing too much blood to continue at this punishing pace. Before she could think of her next steps Fury again charged her, she stumbled back, the tip of his sword catching her cheek. She instinctively put her arm up, wiping her cheek, blotches of blood soaking through her shirt, and streams flowing from the vertical slice of her cheek onto the front of her shirt. Fury's pace of attack was slowing, giving her time to catch her breath as she held Fury's gaze. He charged at her again, Sofia thrusted her sword into his bulging gut, pushed it in further, twisting it for good measure; blood gushing from the wound once she pulled the sword out. Black Fury fell to his knees, Sofia took out her mom's dagger, "This is for my mother and all the torment you caused!" She uttered, gazing into his eyes, as she stabbed him through the heart. He fell to the side, dead!

Sofia, wounded, fell to her knees, tears flowing but not for the death of the most infamous, vile pirate to ever walk the earth but for the end of her quest. She grabbed her dagger from Fury's lifeless body, even more grotesque covered in blood, she thought. She wiped the blood and guts on a piece of burlap sack inches from her, pulled the orb from his pocket and made her way to the open door. She returned the dagger to its sheath and picked up her sword. Men were locking swords as far as her eyes could see, in every direction, hundreds of them.

She scanned the field looking for familiar faces, her eyes fixed on a sizable black man. "Apollo!" She uttered, breathing a sigh of relief.

His reputation proceeding him as a warrior in battle; she watched as Fury's men made failed attempt after failed attempt in striking down the famed Black Ghost. Sofia swallowed hard, eyeing six men in a combined effort, surrounding him. She took a step back, fearing for him. Although her vision still slightly blurred, she saw why Apollo was legend, as he slayed all 6 men where they stood.

Sofia blinked a couple of times, opening her eyes as wide as they would open, catching glimpses of what she was surprised to see were Wayan and Marta. *I can do this*, she thought to herself, *I can go and join them.*

A streak of envy washed through her. She wasn't used to sitting out battles, especially ones she led her people into. There was a difference between the men battling without her and other women battling without her. Her hand gripping the orb lost its grip and the orb fell to the floor. As she bent down to retrieve it from the dirt, she felt the blood trickle down to the base of her back, and the more she moved the more blood flowed. She stabbed the tip of her sword against the ground to steady herself.

Although not in her nature, she surrendered to her injuries; feeling slightly defeated, she staggered at a snail's pace back to the dwelling.

She was only a few paces from the doorway when she caught a glimpse of a man making his way towards her. His sword dripping blood from his latest victim. Her eyes still slightly out of focus, she retreated inside the doorway and prepared to face her oncoming attacker. She attempted to lift her sword but found the action almost impossible. He was still a good length before he'd get to her and currently distracted with one of Apollo's men.

"Sofia!" She recognized that voice, it was Mac! She took a deep breath and exhaled in relief.

Mac came into view. "You look like death warmed over!" Mac said, staring at her. His anger gone the moment he laid his eyes on her. He moved closer, removed a cloth from her pocket and pushed it against her cheek.

"Fury's dead." She stated slowly, lifting the orb. She set her sword on the ground and reached for the material around her neck harboring the other orb. Mac helped her wrap the orb with the other and hung it back around her neck. The final piece; the rebirth of The Futurists and end to the global dominance of Black Fury.

"You're bleeding down your back, did you not notice?" Mac said, setting his sword against the wall. He grabbed the cloth he'd used to wipe Sofia's cheek and stuffed it down the back of her shirt. She moaned and jerked forward from the pain.

"It's all right, I've faired far better than old Fury!" She said, with a slight laugh.

"I'm glad you find this amusing." he started, "If we had not come, you'd be dead by now, not by his hands but by his men!"

"I knew you'd come." She said, plainly, smiling as she turned to face him. "I didn't know Apollo was coming."

"He showed up on *The Margola* after Jessiah, Hugh, Benny and Red came looking for you. He knew the way!" Mac confirmed.

"Red, where is he? Is he away from the fighting?" Sofia asked, in a panic.

"He's fine, I left him in the ravine bed. With instructions to stay there until the fighting is done." He said, pressing the cloth against her wound, making her back muscles convulse under the strain. Sofia caught movement from the corner of her eye, pressed her finger to her lips, slightly pointing to the side. Mac nodded, grabbing his sword, as two men came charging at them. He killed one instantly; the other, was a large, muscular man, skilled in the art of the sword. Sofia retrieved the dagger, holding it backwards by the hilt, she squinted, lining up her shot. The man spun around, back facing Sofia, and without hesitation she flicked her wrist, and the dagger flew into the man's back, forcing him forward, his face just missing Mac's feet.

"What in the world were you thinking? You could have hit me!" He stuttered, shocked and bewildered.

"I've been practicing!" Her eyes glistened and the corners of her mouth slowly turned upwards, in a mischievously coordinated response! "Get my dagger, will you!" She ordered. He grabbed the knife out of the man's back, turning to the field, feeling a sense of duty to the men still battling. "Go!" She ordered, recognizing that need to fight side by side with the men.

Mac handed her the dagger and helped her back through the doorway. "Stay out of sight until I come for you!" He said. She nodded, too weak to argue. He dashed out onto the field, landing next to Jessiah.

The fighting went on for what seemed like hours to Sofia, resting on the ground close to the doorway since Mac left; hearing the sounds of battle, wishing she were standing amongst it. The sounds of swords slapping, battle cries, and occasional gun fire gradually slowed to a stop. Sofia took a deep breath; placed her hands flat on the wall behind her, rising, unstable, but upright. Gradually, she stepped out, surveying the field. Men strewn across the large grassy area as far as her blurry eyes could see, streaks, blotches and pools of red blood spread throughout the vast area. Glancing upwards streams of tears uncontrollably and gently fell from her eyes; the sky, a true antithetical image from the field. An artistic wonder showcasing the real power of mother nature's creative abilities; she marveled at the florescent pink, stark white and luminous orange seemingly enveloping the ordinary brilliant blue sky. *It was a sign*, she thought, *a sign of the clouds of Fury's rein parting, allowing their future to shine as brilliantly as the sun.*

"That's a sight!" She said out loud sheer joy in her voice. Walking towards her, side by side were

Apollo, Ishmael, Mac, Hugh, Benny Wayan, Marta and Tobias.

"Tobias?" She whispered. The small quiet man had a few blood stains on his shirt from the battle. Although he wasn't typically a fighter, his appearance confirmed her belief that he was every bit as dangerous as if he were a great swordsman.

"How did the men fair?" She asked stepping out into the open, Mac a couple of feet from her, the rest several yards behind.

"Jessiah and Apollo's healers are taking stock now." Mac said, stepping behind her, checking the wound in her back. "Some were skilled and worthy adversaries; others were bodies yielding swords." He added, retrospectively. She made a noise of contentment in her throat, as Mac led her back inside.

"Good to see you alive, Captain! My boy and I thank you for what you did here!" Tobias tipped his hat at Sofia, no show of emotion but words of gratitude and started taking stock of the contents in the small dwelling.

"I brought him, I figured Fury would have a decent amount of plundered goods," Said Apollo, sensing the confusion on Sofia's face. She nodded, then eyed Tobias; going about his business, as the expert he was.

"I didn't know you would be here," she said, looking over at Apollo.

"I am simply the protector; you are the avenger! You were born to kill Fury and restore The Futurists; time will show that." The Black Ghost turned to Sofia, smiling tenderly. What a contradiction, Sofia thought; a man so deadly he could be the devil himself yet so honorable, so caring, the contradiction almost too wide for her mind to bridge.

Sofia sat on the floor, watching Tobias work, the small man armed with a quill and paper, feverishly jotting down notes as he quickly worked his way through the piles.

"Captain!" Jessiah, crouched down beside her before she realized he had entered, with Red following moments later. "That's a nasty cut you've got there!" Jessiah said casually, replacing Mac's blood-soaked cloth with one he retrieved from a medical box. The new cloth was soaked in spirits to ward off infection.

She bit her lip, bloody, as shots of pain radiating through her body from the sting of alcohol.

"Jed, you do that again and so help me I'll run you through!" She hissed, blood seeping from her lip, holding up the dagger still clutched in her hands.

"You'll need stitching! I need to stop the bleeding. Apollo's healer gave me some ointment, helpful for healing and infection." He added, paying no mind to her threats.

"Take her back to *The Margola*; we'll care for your wounded and you can come for your men once they've recovered. Tobias is nearly done." Apollo commanded in his deep, melodic voice.

"I want our half of Fury's bounty!" Sofia said, mustering the strength to sound her usual self.

"Of course, do you think I'd cheat the slayer of the infamous Black Fury?" The corners of Apollo's mouth went up, "I'll have it for you when you come for your men." He added, as he nodded to Ishmael, who appeared in the archway of the opening.

"Your able-bodied men are gathered and waiting just outside." Ishmael informed the small group huddled around Sofia. Jessiah and Mac bent down, reaching under her armpits, pulling her to her feet slowly. She pushed at them to stand on her own but her legs gave way, both men catching her by the arms, an inadvertent sound of pain coming from their intolerable patient.

"Take her before she kills herself!" Apollo commanded, with a sternness detected in his voice. Mac nodded as he and Jessiah grabbed Sofia; Red stepping through the archway first, leading them back to *The Margola*.

They stopped several times, allowing Sofia to rest. While Mac and Jessiah's efforts to stem the blood loss helped, the accumulated loss over the hours had taken its' toll. They reached *The Margola* in the black of night, greeted by Mr. Longfellow, who was perched on a stack of sacks staring into the blackness.

"Mr. Longfellow, Get the gangplank down, the Captain is injured!" Yelled Mac, shattering the eerie quiet of midnight. The gangplank barely touched land when Mac and Jessiah were a good two-thirds across, Sofia moaning in discomfort, on the verge of losing consciousness.

"Is she all right?" Longfellow asked, turning on heel to lead them to the Captain's cabin.

"Aye, she will be!" Jessiah answered, strain in his voice as she was dense with muscles and about as tall as most men, even taller than some.

"Mr. Longfellow, my medical bag…" he hadn't needed to finish his sentence, as Mr. Longfellow was gone to retrieve it from the ship's sick room.

"I want to sit up as you stitch me up!" Sofia protested, dagger still clenched in her hand. "Jed!" She yelled through clinched teeth, becoming more difficult to deal with.

"I hear you, Sofia!" Jessiah insisted, sternly. He caught Sofia's eyes, he had never once called her by her first name, she was more shocked than angry, sitting still as he threaded the needle. "Allow me to concentrate or this is not going to end well for either of us!"

"Ah…ouch!" She moaned, as the needle went into her skin, criss-crossing her six-inch gash. She fought the urge to lose consciousness, refusing to give Fury that final satisfaction.

"One more." Jessiah announced, as he looked at his fine stitching work with pride. "I've been getting a fair amount of practice lately." He added, placing the ointment given to him by Apollo's healer on top of Sofia's back. Wayan came into the cabin, holding the two orbs.

Sofia, recovering from Jessiah's handy work, gazed over at Wayan, eyes settling on the orbs.

Sofia turned her head slightly in Mac's direction. "Help me get this from around my neck." Mac grabbed the cloth at her collar bone and lifted the material housing the orbs gently above her head. Wayan set the two down on the table in front of Sofia.

"Let's see what happens." she whispered and Mac set the other two down inches from the others. There was a clicking noise and flashes of a dull light, as the orbs moved, like magnets repelling one another, forming a circle. Within the circle swirled something resembling a witch's brew Sofia thought. It lasted several minutes before they stopped and went dark.

Mac glanced at the still glass balls resting on the table. Sofia, unable to find the strength to keep her eyes open, leaned forward onto her pillow. Mac, Jessiah and Wayan left the room for her to rest.

❀ ❀ ❀

Sofia woke to a concentrated beam of light. It must have only been a few hours of lost consciousness because she was lying on her stomach, same clothes she was sewn in; so sore she used her legs to get to her knees and slowly rose from there. She carefully made her way over to the source of the light; the orbs! Sofia's eye's mesmerized by the movement in the center of the four orbs! Her eyes narrowed as she focused her eyes, images of battles flashed before her; swords striking, blasting of guns, the flow of blood as the final image before they went dark.

"Impending War!" She uttered.

CPSIA information can be obtained
at www.ICGtesting.com
Printed in the USA
LVHW081743090421
683999LV00029B/309

9 781736 8569